T0032486

The Stolen Daughter

Also by ReShonda Tate Billingsley

More to Life

Published by Kensington Publishing Corp.

ReShonda Tate
BILLINGSLEY

The
Stolen
Daughter

KENSINGTON PUBLISHING CORP.
www.kensingtonbooks.com

DAFINA BOOKS are published by

Kensington Publishing Corp.
119 West 40th Street
New York, NY 10018

All Kensington titles, imprints, and distributed lines are available at special quantity discounts for bulk purchases for sales promotion, premiums, fund-raising, and educational or institutional use.

Special book excerpts or customized printings can also be created to fit specific needs. For details, write or phone the office of the Kensington Sales Manager: Kensington Publishing Corp., 119 West 40th Street, New York, NY 10018. Attn. Sales Department. Phone: 1-800-221-2647.

Dafina and the Dafina logo Reg. U.S. Pat. & TM Off.

ISBN-13: 978-1-4967-2414-4
ISBN-10: 1-4967-2414-3
First Kensington Trade Paperback Printing: June 2020

ISBN-13: 978-1-4967-2415-1 (ebook)
ISBN-10: 1-4967-2415-1 (ebook)
First Kensington Electronic Edition: June 2020

10 9 8 7 6 5 4 3 2 1

Printed in the United States of America

Chapter 1

I could never get tired of Luther Vandross, especially this version of the duet that he did with my mother. Or rather that she did with him. Luther's melodic crooning mixed in with my mother's off-key singing was the best sound I ever heard.

"Come on, sweet pea. *Dance with your mother again.*"

My mother had created her own personal duet with Luther, and she was belting out her favorite song, of course substituting a few words.

I set my eight-month-old daughter, Destiny, in her swing, turned on the winding button that was always the first step in putting her to sleep, then smiled as it began its slow swaying back and forth. Destiny giggled in delight—I don't know if it was from the swing or from watching my mother dancing. Either way, both sights brought me immeasurable joy.

"*How I'd love, love, love to dance with my mother again,*" my mother sang as she swayed to the music.

"It's a good thing you chose a career in nursing because we would've starved if you were a singer," I said, laughing as she twirled around.

My mother pulled my arm toward her, trying to get me to join her. "It's a good day. Come on, Jill, and dance with me before you find yourself saying, 'I wish I could dance with my mother again.'"

It's moments like these that made my heart smile. Moments when she could remember. When I saw glimpses of her old self.

She released my arm when she realized I wasn't joining her, then she swayed her hips as her naturally silver curls bounced along with the beat.

My mother's joy was contagious because I found myself saying, "I'd be honored to dance with my mother again." I took her hand and twirled around the small living room of our two-bedroom town house. My mother was right. Today was a good day. She had awakened fully lucid, and after cleaning and preparing lunch, she just wanted to dance.

I swung around and around with her, her giggles rejuvenating me and making me forget about the hard day at work today.

Then suddenly, she stopped, darted over to the fireplace, and picked up the picture frame of my father in his military uniform that I kept over the fireplace mantle. "Here," she said, handing me the eight-by-ten picture. "Dance with your father."

"Mom," I protested, only because memories of missing the father I never knew wasn't a journey I wanted to take today.

"Fine." She held the picture close to her chest and waltzed across the room. I'd seen that sight many times. The love my mother had for my father was unlike anything I'd ever seen. She spoke so fondly of him that I wished that I could steal some of her memories. My dad had died when I was just a baby, so I didn't remember anything about him. But I loved hearing my mother's stories of how he held her hand as I came into this world. How he'd taken one look at me and proclaimed that his life was complete.

They'd given me the name Jillian Jaye after my dad's late mother, and she said that little act only made him love me even more.

"Mom, you're going to wear yourself out," I said as she continued twirling and waltzing. Waltzing and twirling.

She stopped and I could tell that she had gotten a little dizzy. But she caught her bearings and then continued twirling. Slow. Then fast. Then faster.

"Mom. Stop," I said. Her dress made a swishing sound as she turned around and around.

"Mom!" I grabbed her by her arms to stop her because she was twirling uncontrollably. She swayed a bit, then her eyes met mine and my heart sank as the empty expression filled her face.

"Uh . . . uh . . ." she stuttered, then shook her head like she was trying to get clarity. "Who are you?"

"It's me, Mom. Jill," I said, my voice low and soft as I ran my hands up and down her arms, trying to keep her from getting worked up.

"Jill?" Her brow furrowed and I swallowed the lump in my throat.

"Yes. Your daughter."

She bit down on her bottom lip like she was trying to remember. "I don't have a daughter," she finally said. "My baby died."

"I didn't die, Mom." I lifted her chin, hoping if she looked into my eyes she would see what dementia was trying to snatch away.

She took two steps back. "You're not mine." She wagged her finger at me. "Why are you lying? The Lord took my baby."

I smiled, even though the tears were now clouding my view. "I'm yours. I'm your daughter."

Dementia had come into our home like a thief in the night, setting up residence as if I had laid out the welcome mat. The illness had stolen my mother's mind and destroyed my joy as collateral damage.

My mother scooted up against the wall, her blank expression now replaced with fear. "No. Go back to where you came from before the people get me." She shooed me away. "Go. Go!"

"This is my home, Mother," I said, my voice cracking. "You live here with me and Malcolm, and your granddaughter, Destiny." I pointed to the swing, where Destiny was staring at us wide-eyed, like she, too, was shocked by the unfolding scene.

"I don't know a Malcolm or Destiny." Her eyes bulged as she saw the highchair sitting at the kitchen table. "Why is that here?"

"It's Destiny's, Mama. That's my baby. Your granddaughter. You know that," I repeated. "You just fed her lunch in that highchair."

"No. That's here to haunt me." Her eyes grew even wider as she backed up closer to the wall. "That's why it's here." She stared at the highchair like it was about to come to life at any moment and snatch her into an alternate universe.

I eased toward her, my arms outstretched in an effort to calm her down. "You know what, Mama? We've danced enough. You're tired. Why don't you go lie down?"

She kept shaking her head, but she didn't move as I wrapped an arm around her shoulder.

"Someone is torturing me," she mumbled as I led her up the stairs and down the hallway into the tiny bedroom next to ours. I'd hoped this was going to be Destiny's room and I'd had all these grandiose ideas of how I was going to transform the drab, gray walls into a vibrant yellow. But we'd had to transform the room when my mother came to live with us a few months ago.

"My baby died. It was so sad," my mother muttered as I directed her over to the bed. "She just stopped breathing in my womb. I don't know you."

I fought off the tears. My mother was just fifty years old, but the doctors had said dementia didn't discriminate, wasn't limited only to those in their eighties and beyond. I was stunned when another doctor told me people could get early-onset dementia as early as their thirties. And I was even more shocked that out of billions of people in the world, only two hundred thousand in America had early-onset dementia, and my mother was one of them.

Over the last six months, it had attacked my mother with a vengeance. It had stolen her mind, her vitality, and had aged her twenty years. It hurt my heart to watch her transformation.

"No, I didn't die, Mama." I gently eased her down onto her bed. Thankfully, she let me help her lie down.

"One day your mother will come," she said as I pulled the plush blanket up over her shoulders.

"You're my mother," I calmly replied.

"They're going to be really mad," she continued. "They're going to want you back."

I remembered how my mother's doctor had told me that many people with dementia will have psychotic symptoms. "She might believe things that are not real. She also might see, hear, or feel things that are not real. She might argue with you if you try to reason with her," he'd told me. That's exactly what my mother was doing.

I sighed, then just decided to let her live in her fantasy world for a moment.

"And when she comes, I'll tell her Connie Ann Harrison is my mother," I said.

My mother paused as her eyebrows scrunched up again. "Wait. Is that me?"

I nodded with a smile. "All day, every day."

"So is your last name Harrison?" my mother asked.

"It is and always will be. Though it's also Reed, because I married my husband, Malcolm Reed three years ago," I explained. "But you are definitely my mother."

She hesitated, then said, "If I'm your mother . . ."

". . . Then I'm your daughter," I said, completing her sentence.

Her eyes darted up like she was thinking, then she relaxed. "Yes. You're my daughter. Mine. I've known that from the very beginning. God meant for you to be mine."

I didn't understand her rambling; I just wanted to comfort her however I could. That's what she had done for me all my life. Now it was my turn.

My mother took my hand. "And you'll never leave me?"

"Never. Ever." I fluffed her pillow and she snuggled into it like it had taken her into a warm embrace.

"I can sleep now. My daughter will never leave me," she muttered.

I was thankful for her room-darkening curtains. The September sun was on full blast and I needed all her nerves to be at peace so that she could rest.

I leaned over, kissed my mother on the forehead, and assured her that I would never go anywhere. Then I turned out the lights, eased out of her room, and cried.

Chapter 2

Caregiving was no joke. I'd finally gotten my mother settled and was grateful to walk back in the living room and find Destiny dozing off in her swing. That Goodwill find had been a blessing because my baby girl absolutely loved it.

I turned the swing off, then eased Destiny out and took her upstairs to take a nap in the crib we'd set up in our bedroom. That gave me just the break I needed to try and see if I could get dinner ready before Malcolm came home.

I had just finished cooking fettuccini alfredo when I heard the key in the door turn. As the door eased open, I immediately noticed how my husband's six foot two frame was slumped over. The expression on his face revealed the fact that his job interview hadn't gone well.

"Hey, babe," I said.

"Hey," he replied, dropping his keys on the table by the door. I took in how sexy he looked, even though he was wearing a Suit Mart suit that looked a size too big. I think it was his dimples, shining brightly even when he was upset. He looked just like a younger Rick Fox, though he hated when anyone made the comparison.

"So, when do they want you to start?" I said, hoping my optimistic smile would make him smile. It didn't.

"I'm not going to get the job. I'm underqualified," he snapped. "You know I might as well not have gone to college at all versus dropping out," he moaned. "Maybe if I had spent those two years working on my app, I wouldn't even need a job because I'd be rich."

I suppressed the sigh that was itching to escape. My husband and this app had been the bane of my existence. He was convinced he had the next big thing. It was a travel app that used location services to tell you all the best places to dine, shop, party, and chill, no matter where you were. And it was tailored to your individual tastes and budget. He also had several other components that were way too complicated for me to understand. He'd been working on this since apps were a thing. Don't get me wrong, I believed in him, but dreams didn't put food into Destiny's stomach. Dreams didn't keep a roof over our head. Truthfully, a part of me wondered if Malcolm was self-sabotaging when it came to finding a job. He'd worked as a maintenance engineer, which wasn't nearly as sexy as it sounded. Basically, my husband was one step above a janitor/handyman. And he hated every minute of it. I think he was secretly happy about being laid off. At the time, anyway, he had been confident that his app would have taken off by now.

Malcolm loosened the tie that I knew he hated putting on in the first place. "I'm sick of this. I don't know how they expect a brother to get ahead when nobody will take a chance on you. I'm not asking for a handout. I'm asking for a chance. I'm twenty-nine years old, out here slumming like I'm nineteen."

"We are not slumming, babe. Yes, we struggle. But we have a roof over our heads, so we're blessed."

"Yeah, a leaky roof in a dump of an apartment complex that they call townhomes, like that's supposed to make it better," he snapped. "The people next door sell drugs. The ones downstairs put Ike and Tina Turner to shame. And I swear the lady across the hall is running a brothel. Yeah, this is exactly the life I envisioned for us," he added, his voice dripping with sarcasm.

I turned the fire down and let the alfredo sauce simmer, then walked over to try and hug my husband. His body remained tense. I rubbed his arm trying to soothe him. "It's going to be okay," I whispered. "*We're* going to be okay."

He wiggled from my grasp. "How, Jill? My wife is working as a barista at Starbucks," he said.

"Starbucks has good benefits. Plus, I get my Grande Mocha Frappuccino at a discount. Do you know how much that saves me?" I replied, once again forcing a smile even though I'd just had this conversation with myself on the way home from work. I was thinking the same thing as Malcolm—this is not where I saw my life at twenty-seven.

"Starbucks is for college kids. The deal was, you were supposed to stay home and take care of Destiny for the first two years," he said, exasperated. I noticed the worry lines that had begun creeping up on his smooth chocolate skin. He'd found a gray hair last week and almost lost his mind. I knew all of that was nothing but stress.

"I want more for us," he continued. "If I could just get someone to believe in this app, I know it would be a success and I could give you the life I promised you."

I pulled my husband close. This time, he didn't jerk away.

"From the moment we met, I promised to make you happy," he said, dejected.

"And you've done just that," I told him, stroking his soft, naturally curly hair.

"But we shouldn't be struggling like this. You shouldn't be working in a coffee shop."

"Well, life happens, baby. So, I'm doing what I have to do," I said, standing on my tiptoes to kiss him. I would never tell Malcolm this, but I did regret quitting my job as a receptionist for Blue Cross Blue Shield of Texas, a large healthcare company. Quitting had been something Malcolm had wanted me to do when Destiny was born. His mother had been a stay-at-home mother, and that's what he wanted for his children. But three weeks after Destiny's one-month birthday, Malcolm had been laid off from his job as a maintenance engineer supervisor at Houston Community College. And things had never returned to normal.

While I wanted more, I didn't detest the Starbucks job because it was decent money and it gave me benefits for my family, but something about me working there bothered my husband to no end. It was probably because he was from a traditional family; his own mother hadn't worked and had spent her life raising Malcolm and his three sisters. While I had agreed to stay at home for a while, that wasn't going to be me forever. My hope was that when Destiny started kindergarten, I'd be able to go back to school and finish my degree. I didn't know how in the world I would pay for it and with each passing day, I started to wonder if I was too old. But that was on my bucket list.

"How long before dinner is ready?" Malcolm asked, throwing up his hands like he just wanted to change the subject.

"I'm almost done, sweetie. By the time you get changed the garlic bread will be done."

"Where's Destiny? Asleep?"

Before I could answer, we heard our daughter's cries. Both Malcolm and I turned our attention to the kitchen entrance.

"Oh my God!" Malcolm screamed.

My mother was standing there, holding Destiny upside down by her legs.

"Mom," I said, racing over toward her. But Malcolm had already reached her and retrieved the baby from her arms.

"The baby was crying," my mother said. She had a zombie-like expression that tore at my heart.

"You shouldn't carry her," I said, examining Destiny, who was still crying as she snuggled close to her father's chest.

"Why not? I know how to carry a baby," my mother replied.

Malcolm glared at me as he clutched our wailing daughter to his chest. His unspoken words belied his fury.

"Come on, Mom. Let me get you back in your room," I said, once I saw Malcolm had settled our daughter.

"I'm hungry. Is it time for Thanksgiving dinner?" My mother had three expressions since she'd gotten sick: confused, blank, and what I called lost. Right now, she was confused. Her confusion had become a daily companion rather than an infrequent visitor.

"It's September, Mommy. No Thanksgiving dinner yet. But regular dinner will be ready in a little bit. Why don't you go watch *Family Feud* until it's done?" I knew that I needed to get her out of my husband's presence before he did something we all would regret. He loved my mother, but it was nothing compared to his love for our daughter.

"Oooh, I like *Family Feud*," my mother said, a wide grin spreading across her face.

"I know."

"I like that host, Richard Dawson."

"But now it's Steve Harvey," I gently replied.

"Who is Steve Harvey?"

"That's the bald black man with the bushy mustache," I said as I led her toward the stairs. "Mommy, what did we talk about with Destiny?"

"I don't know," she said, shrugging.

"You can't hold her unless one of us is present."

"But I hold her all the time."

"Yes, but since you've been sick, you promised to only hold her when someone else was around."

"Okay," she said, her tone soft, like a child being chastised.

I got my mother tucked back in her bed, put the TV show on and went back downstairs, preparing to face the wrath of my husband. And he did not disappoint.

"Before you say anything," I said, holding my hands up because I could feel the fury coming from his body.

"Jill . . ." he growled.

"Babe, I know. I talked to her. She knows she's not supposed to handle Destiny," I said.

"It looks like she doesn't know much of anything," he snapped.

I felt tears welling up. We'd been having this argument a whole lot lately but I didn't know what else he expected me to do. I was my mother's only child. And she was her mother's only child, so our family was small. Her mother had died when she was in high school and she had one aunt, Marilyn, who was too old to take her. It's not like my mother had anywhere else to go.

As I looked at my husband, I knew what he expected me to do because he'd told me on more than one occasion.

"It's time, Jill. This place is too small, and your mother needs full-time care." His voice was calmer now.

"Would you put your mother in a home?" I said, knowing he wouldn't.

"We're not talking about my mother. If she was a threat to our child, then yes," he added, brushing Destiny's hair as she sucked on her two fingers.

"Mama isn't a threat," I protested.

He looked at me like I was crazy. "She just walked in here holding our baby upside down."

"I know, but—"

"There's no buts," he said, cutting me off. "This is crazy. Your mother is sick. And I know on some days, she's fine. But some days she's not. And one of these days, she could be dangerous.

You're not going to be happy until she's done some serious damage to our child." He turned to storm out of the room.

"Are you not going to eat?" I said, only because I didn't know what else to say.

"I've lost my appetite," he said as he clutched our daughter and went back upstairs.

Chapter 3

Please Lord, don't let me get fired.

That's all I could think as I whipped into a parking spot, threw my Ford Festiva into park, grabbed my green apron, and raced inside.

"Shoot," I muttered when I saw the long line. Whoever invented Starbucks had hit a gold mine because it was always busy. I knew caffeine was an addiction but the lines in Starbucks took it to a whole other level. The bad thing was, the twenty-deep line was going to get me in trouble. The good thing? The twenty-deep line kept my boss from going off on me.

"Sorry, Tony," I said as I threw my apron around my neck and tied it in the back.

"Can you just get over there and help Sandra? The drive-thru is backed up," he barked.

"Yes, sir."

I knew Tony was beyond ready to fire me. I'd been late every day this week. After my mom's dangling Destiny episode, things had progressively gotten worse. I never knew what I would wake up to. When I first took my mother to the doctor after she started acting strange, they actually tried to tell me nothing was wrong. But I knew something was wrong. Any doctor that wasn't on Medicaid could see something was wrong. But you get what you pay for. And since we paid nothing at the free clinic, that's exactly what we got in return. It wasn't until a doctor from her church agreed to see her that we got a proper diagnosis. I couldn't help but wonder if maybe we had gotten her some help at the first sign of her illness, maybe it wouldn't have progressed so quickly.

No sense in dwelling in maybes now. I picked up a cup. "Is this one for the drive-th . . ." Before I could finish my sentence, the cup slipped from my hand and splattered to the floor.

"Seriously?" Tony screamed. My coworker, Angie, jumped out of the way but it was too late, the coffee had burned her arm.

"Owwwww!" she wailed. Angie was so extra, she knew that coffee wasn't that dang hot. But knowing her drama queen performance, she would go to the hospital and take three weeks off.

"Sorry," I muttered. I ignored Angie screaming like someone was burning her cornea with a cigarette, grabbed a towel, and started trying to wipe the mess up off the floor.

"Get her to the back," Tony yelled to the guy on the register. "Jill, can you take an order without messing that up?"

I hated being publicly chastised and couldn't wait for the day when I could tell Tony what I thought about his rude tone. But since I needed this job, I just nodded and stepped to the register.

"Sorry for the delay," I told the customer. "May I help you?"

Before the petite brunette could speak, my phone rang. I silently cursed the fact that I'd forgotten to turn the ringer off. I eased it out of my pocket, planning to simply shut it off.

No, no, no, I thought when I saw my mother's cell phone number on the screen.

"Come on, Jill. Get the line moving," Tony called out from the espresso machine he was trying to fix.

I pushed ignore, turned the ringer off, and took the woman's complicated order. *Did anyone come in Starbucks and order plain black coffee?*

The customer had just scanned her Starbucks app when my phone vibrated. I tried to ignore it as the next customer gave me their order, but it just kept loudly vibrating. What if it was an emergency? What if something had happened to Mama and someone was trying to get in touch with me?

"Excuse me," I said to the man who had just stepped to my register. "I'm sorry. I have to get this. It must be an emergency." I hunched down and cupped my mouth to the phone. "Hello?"

"Jill!" I groaned, because it wasn't an emergency.

"What, Mama? You know I'm at work," I whispered.

"Jill, I can't find the apartment!" My mother was hysterical as her voice bellowed through the phone.

"What do you mean you can't find the apartment?" I said.

The man cleared his throat and I held up one finger asking him to hold on. I glanced back at Tony, who thankfully was busy struggling with the machine.

"They moved it. They moved the apartment." She started sobbing.

"Okay, Mama. I need you to take a deep breath. Where are you?" I whispered.

"I just needed some fresh air and I went for a walk. When I came back, they had moved the apartment." I could hear the panic in her voice.

I massaged my temples. "Okay. You know the apartment number is 3749?"

"Yes. That's where I am."

"Okay then, Mama. Have you used your key?"

"I didn't lock the door." She huffed, then released a loud sob.

I sighed. We didn't have much, but I didn't want someone to steal it.

"Mama, is the apartment yellow?"

A pause, then she said, "No. It's burgundy."

I took a deep breath. "Mama, you did this last week. Those are the apartments next door. We live in the yellow ones next to that."

"We do?"

"Yes. So go to the yellow apartments next door, then go up to the third floor, make a right and go down to number 3749. Call me when you get inside."

"Can't you stay on the phone with me?" she whimpered.

"I can't because I'm at work." A sickening feeling filled my insides. I didn't want to leave Malcolm with the burden of caring for my mom, so I usually sent her with my great-aunt or dropped her off at the adult day care facility. Occasionally, I left her home alone. Now, it seemed like that option would no longer be feasible.

"Okay," she said. I could hear the fear in her voice. I was going to have to break down and get her some help at home, but how in the world was I going to afford that?

"Call me when you get in the house, okay?" I told her.

"Okay, thank you, baby. I don't know what I would do without you. I love you."

"I love you, too, Mama."

I hung up to see Tony standing over me. "Really, Jill? You're late, then you come in and get on the phone?"

"I'm so sorry. It was an emergency."

"It always is. I am sick and tired of you and your emergencies." His voice was loud and now everyone was staring at me.

"You're the most emergencies-having person I've ever seen," he snapped.

"I said I was sorry." I kept my voice low in hopes that he would lower his.

"I'm tired of you, and your sorries, too."

"I don't know what else you want me to do," I said, the weight of everything taking its toll on me. I took the apron off and threw it on the ground. "Fine, you want me out? I'm gone."

I stomped around the corner, keenly aware that I'd tossed my "I don't like to draw attention" mantra out of the window with this scene. But I was tired of the stress of everything.

"Jill, stop overreacting. Nobody said they wanted you out. I just want you to do your job without all the extra drama," he called out after me.

All eyes in the place were on me but I didn't care. I just needed to get out of there before I lost it. The whole week had been overwhelming.

"I'm sorry, Tony . . . I'm losing it," I said, before turning to race out the door.

Just as I swung the door open, I bumped into one of our regulars. "Oh, excuse me. I'm sorry. Mr. Logan, right?"

He nodded. "I told you last week to call me Major."

He'd been coming in almost every other day for the past month. His warm smile was familiar and made my anxiety relax—just a bit.

"Are you okay?" he asked when he noticed my misty eyes and frazzled demeanor.

"Yes, rough day." I glanced back inside the store and saw Tony had stepped up to work the register.

"So, you're not going to be able to make my tall, soy, no-water chai?" Mr. Logan asked with a smile.

I shook my head as I fought back tears. "No, someone else will take care of you." I wanted to add, "permanently," because I was sure I was fired.

"But I don't like the way they make it," he protested as he winked at me.

I managed a smile. If I didn't know better, I'd swear this old man was flirting with me, because every time he came in, he was extra nice. The first few times, I noticed him just staring at me. Then, he started making small talk. I imagined if I were thirty years older, I'd find his salt and pepper beard and tailored clothes attractive.

"Are you headed somewhere?" he asked.

"I-I . . ." I choked back the rest of my sentence. How would I explain to Malcolm that I had walked out of my job? He didn't want me to work, but he knew like I did that I had to work. No, tomorrow I would have to call Tony and grovel for forgiveness. And my job. "I think I just made my boss furious and I'm probably going to lose my job," I said, swallowing the lump in my throat.

"You know what?" he said. "You need something stronger than coffee. Can I buy you a drink?"

So he *was* flirting with me. "I think you're very nice, Mr. Logan," I said, "but I'm not interested like that."

"Oh, no, no," he exclaimed. "I am very married. Happily. Twenty-eight years. He took a deep breath. "In fact, that's my wife in the car," he continued, pointing to the silver luxury vehicle parked directly in front of us.

"Oh," I said, slightly embarrassed, as the woman waved to me from the back seat. I waved back.

"I was actually coming to see if you were at work today," Mr. Logan said.

"Me?" I asked, turning my attention back to him.

"My wife wanted to meet you."

Now, I frowned. "Well, I'm sorry. I have to leave. I've had a rough day."

"Please? It would mean a lot. It would mean the world to my wife if she had the chance to meet you."

I didn't understand how meeting me would mean anything to this man or his wife.

"I'll go in and talk to your boss." He flashed a smile. "I know the CEO of Starbucks and I assure you, whatever happened, you won't lose your job. Just take a moment, talk to my wife, and I'll go in and talk to the manager."

I paused, looked at the woman in the back of the car, then the man in a suit that was driving. Though I had no idea what they wanted, nothing about them seemed dangerous, and if Mr. Logan could help me keep my job . . .

"Fine," I said, "I'll talk to your wife."

He smiled his gratitude, then walked me over to the car. I opened up the doors—they opened backward like something out of the movies, and I stepped in—wondering what in the world these people wanted.

Chapter 4

Images of Major Logan stayed with me on my drive home. I was still thinking about him when my cell phone rang and I saw my best friend, Cynthia's, name pop up on the screen.

"Hey, girl, what's going on?" I said, after answering the phone.

Cynthia and I had been best friends since middle school. But our lives were so different now. She'd pledged a sorority, graduated from college, and was enjoying the single life while traipsing all over the country in her job as a pharmaceutical sales rep. But we still remained close.

"Just calling to check on you," she sang. "I just got back from Dubai and I'm trying to see what's been going on in your life."

I let out a heavy sigh. "You have no idea. Between work, my mom, Destiny, and Malcolm not being able to find a job, I swear, I need a vacation."

"At least he's given up that app dream."

"Girl, you know he hasn't. He's convinced that that he just needs to make the right connection."

"Well, it is a great idea, but ideas don't pay the bills."

"You're preaching to the choir," I replied.

"I told you that you should've come to Belize with me last month. You need to let your hair down."

"Oh, yeah, because I so have money for that." Cynthia had offered to pay my way, but I wasn't going to be that broke friend. Besides, even if Malcolm could watch Destiny, I couldn't leave my mother.

"So Malcolm is still not having any luck on the job front?" she asked. I pictured her, lying across her sofa, her feet dangling as she enjoyed her carefree life.

"Nope," I replied, pulling into the CVS to pick up some Pampers for Destiny. Well, not Pampers. Since Malcolm had lost his job, we'd gone generic on everything. Now, the diapers we bought were just called "diapers."

"You'd think an auto mechanic-slash-maintenance-slash-handyman-slash-tech guru would be able to find a job," she said. "Malcolm can do everything."

"I know," I said as I made my way into the store. "And he gets odd jobs, but not enough to get and keep us out of debt. He's convinced that if he could just get a small business loan, he'd be set, but neither of us has any real credit."

"Isn't it sad that we never learned about credit growing up?"

"Isn't it sad we don't have the connections to get million-dollar little loans," I added and we both laughed.

Cynthia and I made some more small talk as I bought the diapers and headed back to the car. I had just pulled out of the parking lot when I said, "Oh yeah, let me tell you what happened at work today." After I'd talked to Mrs. Logan, Mr. Logan stayed true to his word, and Tony had allowed me to come back and finish my shift. I don't know what kind of clout he had, but Tony was extra nice to me after that.

"I still can't believe you're working at Starbucks." Cynthia tsked.

"Like I told Malcolm, I gotta do what I gotta do." I turned the corner out of the lot as I began to recap the story. "But listen. So this older man that has been coming in the store all the time asked me to talk to him."

"Oh, hey now," Cynthia sang.

"He looked like he had a whole bunch of money and he had one of those big Rolls Royces where the doors open funny," I continued.

"Oh, now you're about to get a sugar daddy," she said. I could picture my friend getting excited. "Maybe you can get the money to kick start Malcolm's little dream after all." She laughed.

"Will you be quiet and let me finish?"

"I'm just saying."

"Anyway," I continued. "I know this sounds crazy, but he asked if I would mind getting in the car and talking to his wife for a few minutes."

"What?" she exclaimed. All playfulness was gone and her danger meter was on high alert. "And you did? Don't you watch *First 48* or *Snapped* or any of the other thousands of crime shows? Why in the world would you get in his car?"

"Like I said, he's been coming in a while. He seemed pretty harmless."

"I bet Charles Manson seemed harmless at some point, too," she said.

"Look, can I finish my story, please?" I huffed. "I had stormed off work because I have just had a really rough week and I was sure Tony was going to fire me. This man, his name is Mr. Logan, claimed to know the CEO and would go talk to Tony for me if I would talk to his wife."

"I can't believe he wanted you to talk to his wife. And why was she even in the back seat? Okay, is this some kind of freaky stuff they had going on?" I could tell Cynthia's antenna was on high alert. "What did she want to talk to you about? Were they some type of sex cult couple?"

"I seriously don't know what she wanted. She creeped me out. She just sat there staring at me at first. It was so weird. Her eyes were all watery and she just stared at me without saying anything. Then she asked me questions like 'Was I happy in my life?' And 'Did I consider myself well rounded?' It was the weirdest thing ever."

I could hear Cynthia's confusion through the phone. "So, she didn't say why they wanted to talk to you?"

"No," I replied.

"She just pummeled you with questions?"

"Yes."

"Okay, that's for real creepy," Cynthia said.

"She did offer me a Coke, and she kept insisting that I drink it."

"A Coke? Oh my God. They probably were going to drug you and kidnap you," Cynthia exclaimed.

"No, I never got that vibe. It kind of felt like they were . . . I don't know, maybe they were just some lonely old people," I said. "But it was really weird."

"That is strange." Cynthia pounced into mother mode. "Look here, don't go getting into cars with strange people. I have a full calendar and do not have time to go to a funeral." That was my best friend, forever the protector.

"Well, I didn't think he was strange because he's come in Starbucks many times over the last couple of months," I replied. "He seems like a nice enough guy."

"Again, most killers don't wear name tags," Cynthia said. "The bottom line is you don't know him, so stay out of his car before you end up on the news."

"You're right," I said as I pulled into the parking lot of our apartment complex. I turned off the ignition, looked at my town house, and sighed. The dilapidated building with its chipped 1980s yellow paint was not where I wanted to be at this point in my life, but I had to stay faithful that things would turn around for us at some point.

"Well, girl, I'm home," I said to my friend. "Let me get inside. I see Malcolm's truck so I'm going to go in and pray he's in a better mood."

"Okay. Call me later." She paused. "And Jill?" she added.

"Yeah?"

"I'm going to say a prayer that you and Malcolm get a break. Both of you deserve it."

"Thank you, Cyn. I love you," I replied.

"I love you, too."

I hung up and made my way up the walkway, with its broken concrete and weeds peeking through every crack. I carefully stepped over the mounds of red ants that were setting up a new home at the end of the sidewalk, then eased my key in the door, which could easily open with one good kick, and walked in to see Malcolm sitting at the dining room table bouncing our daughter on his lap as he pored over some papers.

"Hey, babe," I said, walking over and kissing him on top of the head first, then kissing our daughter on the cheek. She giggled with delight.

"How was your day?" he said, not looking up. "I thought you didn't get off until nine."

"Fine," I replied, deciding to forego additional details for now. "Is Aunt Marilyn here yet with Mama?"

"Not yet. She called and said they were going to stop by Ross to shop a little." He sighed as he pushed Destiny's hand back from trying to grab the papers. "I'm just sitting here trying to figure out how we're going to pay these bills. They're slated to cut off the lights tomorrow." His words were weighted with frustration and I felt awful for my husband. Being able to care for his family meant a lot to him.

"I get paid on Friday," I told him. "That's in three days."

"The extension is until tomorrow," he said. "I knew I should've told Kendra that I couldn't afford that stupid tux she has me wearing for her wedding this weekend," he said, referring to his sister, who was getting married to her longtime boyfriend. "That money could've paid the light bill." Malcolm blew an exasperated breath as he rubbed his temple. "When is your mom's social security check coming in?"

I hated when he asked about that check. I knew that my husband didn't mean anything malicious by it, but that money was supposed to be for my mom's care. Yet, ever since she'd been here, Malcolm had been finding other things to do with the money. "I don't know, but you know I hate using that money for bills," I said.

He must've sensed my apprehension because he said, "Look, babe, I know you hate using that check for anything other than your mother, but I don't know what will happen if your mother has to sit here in the dark."

I sighed and shrugged. "Well, it's not here yet. They start direct deposit of her check this month, maybe it'll come in tonight."

He took another deep breath. "Let's hope it does, or we all will be sitting in the dark tomorrow."

I didn't know what to say to that so I just walked over to the stove. "Did you cook anything?" I asked, looking around for some sign of dinner. He looked up at me like I was speaking a foreign language and it was my turn to release an exasperated breath. But he was the one at home all day and I was the one working. The least he could do was cook. "I'll order a pizza from Little Caesars. They have that five dollar special," I said after he just kept giving me that blank stare. It was sad that I had to hesitate over a pizza. But I was exhausted and we had to eat, so I decided not to fight it.

Malcolm shrugged and went back to trying to figure out the bills. I grabbed my phone and logged onto the pizza place, ordered one pizza, and then sat down next to him at the table.

"Hey, this guy showed up at work today," I began.

That made him look up and give me his undivided attention. Malcolm wasn't the jealous type when we first met. But he'd been feeling some kind of way about being laid off and I'd been seeing a possessive side of him that was definitely out of the ordinary. Cynthia said Malcolm was probably worried that I would leave him for a man with a good job. Which, of course, was absolutely ludicrous. Since the day Malcolm and I had met, when I took my first jalopy—a 1993 Chevy Chevette—to his uncle's shop, we'd been inseparable. That was seven years ago.

"What guy?" he asked.

"I don't know. Some older man who wanted to talk to me."

He raised an eyebrow. "Talk to you about what?"

"Not like that," I quickly said. "He's a regular customer, comes in all the time. I don't know what he wanted, to be honest. He just was kind of rambling, then he asked me to talk to his wife."

I guess since I had told Malcolm that the man wasn't trying to pick me up, he was no longer interested, because he simply shrugged and said, "You guys meet all kinds in Starbucks," then he stood and handed me Destiny, who was falling asleep in his arms. "Well, look, I'm going to go lie down." He kissed Destiny on the head as she snuggled into my chest. "Looking for a job is almost exhausting as working a job. Then Kendra is stressing me over this wedding on Saturday. She and Travis have two kids. Why they're having a big wedding is beyond me," he moaned. "Anyway, Mike and the boys will be by later. We're going to watch the game."

"They're coming here?" I asked. It's not that I didn't like Malcolm's friends. They were cool. But our town house was too small to be the hangout spot.

"Yeah, Mike's TV is out, and Tyrone lives all the way on the north side." Malcolm looked at me and added, "You probably should call the pizza place back and order some extra pizzas."

I cocked my head at him. Just a minute ago, he was telling me how he didn't know how we were going to keep the lights on because we were so broke. Now, I was supposed to be ordering pizza for his friends?

Before I could say anything, he added, "You think you can keep your mother upstairs while they're here?"

I didn't even feel like arguing. I simply nodded and wondered how much more of this life I could take.

Chapter 5

Kendra Reed might have done things backward—two kids first, then a husband, but her fiancé, Travis, was giving her the wedding of her dreams. That made my heart swell since my sister-in-law and I were extremely close. She'd been a support system for me when Malcolm first lost his job. And she understood my frustration with his "dream-chasing."

Kendra's approval meant the world to me since Malcolm's mother didn't really care for me. She felt like her son could do better, which was ludicrous since it wasn't like they were some well-to-do family and Malcolm was slumming with me. He was from a middle-class working family. The only difference was he'd been raised with two parents while I only had my mother. We'd both dropped out of college. Well, Malcolm always said he dropped out, but really, he flunked out because he spent all of his time developing one idea after another. I dropped out my sophomore year, one of my biggest regrets. But the healthcare company I worked for was paying good money and I had to go full-time or lose the job.

We were currently inside the sanctuary of New Faith Missionary Baptist Church, the church Malcolm and his family had been raised in. Travis's family had spared no expense and the entire sanctuary was adorned with white calla lilies, with silver and purple accents throughout. It was the perfect complement to the rich purple bridesmaids' dresses. It was simply beautiful.

The wedding music began playing and I stood with the rest of the guests. I beamed with pride as I focused my eyes on my beautiful sister-in-law, who had been one of my closest friends before I even knew her brother.

Kendra didn't look like what she'd been through. And that was a good thing. Few twenty-seven-year-olds had had to endure a round of chemotherapy in a fight to save their breast, but she had, and she'd come through like the fighter she was. And today she was marrying the man of her dreams.

Malcolm tried to play hard, but I could tell he was emotional because he winked at me as he stood next to Travis at the altar. I knew that wink was for me because that was Malcolm's term of endearment.

It was simply to tell me to be strong. Malcolm knew that I'd wanted a big wedding, but neither of us had been in a financial position to make that happen. And it wasn't like my mother even had enough to buy the flowers for our wedding, let alone to give us something even close to a formal ceremony.

Kendra's soon-to-be-husband's family was footing the bill for this wedding and that had broken Malcolm's heart. His father had asked that he take care of the family before his death, so he'd dreamed of paying for his only sister's wedding, along with ours. He used to talk about how if one of his ideas would hit, he'd be able to do all of that and more.

Travis's parents hadn't batted an eye when they decided that in welcoming Kendra into their world, she would experience all the joy that came with it. Of course, they'd felt some kind of way about her having children out of wedlock, but once the twins got here, their hearts had melted and they loved Kendra like they'd given birth to her.

The music continued playing and every image of Kendra flickered through my mind as she took the slow stroll down the aisle.

The first time she stuck up for me in ninth grade when the mean girls were calling me a wannabe because of my "light-bright, half-white complexion." The time when Malcolm and I broke up and she let me cry on her shoulder, while never bad-mouthing her brother. The time she comforted me when my mother was first diagnosed with dementia. There were so many memories and I was happy to be here to share in this day with her.

When Kendra got to me, I clutched my hand to my heart to keep my tears at bay. She mouthed, "I love you." Then, instinctively, her eyes went behind me to my mother, and a blanket of worry passed over Kendra's face. I looked over at my mother, who was standing next to me, fidgeting. She was no doubt bothered by the taffeta dress I had insisted she wear. I took my mother's hand to calm her. And she looked up and smiled. That made me smile.

Kendra really cared for my mother and often assisted me with her care. My mother also adored her. I knew my friend wanted my mother here, which is one of the reasons I had opted out of being one of her bridesmaids. I told Kendra that I had to sit with Mama. In actuality, I knew we couldn't afford the dress or any of the other bridesmaid activities and I knew Malcolm would die if I let Kendra or Travis's family pay for it.

"Dearly beloved," the minister began as we all took our seats, "we are gathered here today."

"Mama, sit down," I whispered when she didn't take her seat.

"I don't wanna," my mother said, pulling at the dress around the neck. "Why do I have on this dress? Am I in a beauty pageant?"

I forced a smile and struggled to get her seated as Travis's mother glanced back at us. She'd met my mother last night at the rehearsal dinner and I could tell she had concerns about my mother attending. But I'd assured Kendra that everything would be fine.

"Remember, Mama? Kendra is getting married. You promised you would be on your best behavior," I whispered, hoping my low tone would convince her to whisper, too. It didn't.

"But why do I have to wear this dress?" she said, her voice raising an octave.

"Mama. Shhh," I said.

"Don't shush me. I'm the mama. I mean, I'm your mama now." I had no idea what she was talking about. But these days, I seldom did.

I was mortified. Everyone, including the pastor and Malcolm, was looking at us.

"Okay, if you sit here and be quiet, we'll go look at the blue bonnets afterward," I said.

"Blue bonnets?"

"Yes, remember you like the blue bonnet field on the way home," I said, still whispering.

"Oh, yeah." She smiled.

"So, please just sit here." I patted the seat next to me.

She nodded as she sat back down. Kendra kept looking back over her shoulder. Malcolm's expression had tightened.

"It's fine," I mouthed.

The people that had been looking at us turned their attention back to the front as the minister resumed his spiel. I couldn't really enjoy the ceremony like I wanted to, because I kept my hand clutched with my mother's, fearful that at any moment things would go left.

My joy finally returned when the minister asked everyone to stand as Kendra and her handsome husband turned to face us.

"Ladies and gentlemen, I present to you, Mr. and Mrs. Travis Keith Braxton."

The organist began playing as the crowd erupted in applause. The noise made my mother jump and my hand clutched her tighter.

"Can we go now?" she said, hanging onto my arm like she was terrified.

Thankfully, the organ music was playing loud as Travis and

Kendra began making their exit from the sanctuary. Their six bridesmaids and groomsmen followed close behind.

"Who are all these people?" my mother asked as she looked around the room. I silently willed the organist to play louder.

"It's okay, Mama. I got you."

Thankfully, Mama stayed quiet all the way from the church to the reception. I could tell Malcolm was a little pissed. I caught him taking several glances at my mother in the rear-view mirror.

"She's fine now," I said, placing my hand on my husband's arm. He didn't reply as he kept his eyes on the road.

The reception was at the Marriott Marquis, and it revealed every bit of the Braxton money. Like at the church, there were fresh flowers throughout the venue. We'd taken the escalator up to the ballroom and stepped off to what looked like a winter wonderland in September.

After I got Mama settled at a table, I headed over to the buffet table to get her something to eat. Malcolm's mother stood over the table, shaking her head. "This doesn't even make sense. They probably paid as much as my whole house cost for this shindig."

"It's nice though," I told her as I reached over and put some meatballs on a plate for my mother.

Mrs. Reed pursed her lips as she turned to me, then glanced over at the table where my mother was sitting. "You know, I think you should have listened to Malcolm and left your mother at home."

"I wanted her to share in this day. Besides, Kendra wanted her here," I replied.

I expected my mother-in-law to give me some smart retort, but instead, she set her plate down and took one of my hands. "Sweetie, you're going to have to accept it. Your mother has Alzheimer's."

"She has dementia," I corrected her.

"They're really the same," she continued. "Everybody knows you love her, but this day is too important. It's not about you or your mama. It's about Kendra."

"I understand, but she's good. Besides, we're here now, so—"

"Oh my God." We heard a scream from the other side of the room. "Look at what she did to this two-thousand-dollar cake," I heard Travis's mother scream.

I darted across the room at the same time as Kendra and Travis. The gasps were immediate. My mother was standing there next to the beautiful wedding cake that we had marveled at on the way in. Apparently, Travis's mother had called in some favors to get the world-renowned chef, Clyde Jiles, to make her cake. And now, that big, beautiful cake was missing two huge chunks on both sides. And standing next to the empty spaces was my mother with crumpled up cake in each hand. It looked like she'd taken her palms and dipped them into the cake and snatched two handfuls.

"Mama," I gasped. "What did you do?"

"I wanted cake," she said as she stuffed her mouth with a handful of the buttermilk-white cake icing that surrounded her nose as if she'd smashed the cake in her face.

"Oh my God," Kendra cried as she approached the table.

I felt all eyes bore into me. Malcolm appeared on the side of me, his gaze screaming all kinds of "I told you so." All I could do was mutter my apologies as I tried to get my mother and scurry her out of the room.

"No!" my mother said, snatching away from me. "Let me go. I don't know you!" she screamed. She backed away from me and bumped into the table where the cake was sitting. Before anyone could react, the cake came tumbling down.

"Oh no," she said, reaching for the cake. Of course it was too late. Cake splattered everywhere. "I-I'm so s-sorry," she stammered.

"What did you do?" Travis's mother screamed, all her prim decorum gone.

The outburst caused my mother to turn and race out of the room.

I flashed an apologetic look at all the eyes that were staring at me, then took off after my mother.

"Mama," I called out to her just as she reached the stairs. "Wait!"

But she didn't stop, she put one foot on the top step and the next thing I knew, she was tumbling down the flight of stairs.

Chapter 6

"*So how do I look?*"

I laughed at the sight of my mother with the bushy mustache, the tattered brown suit from Goodwill and the glued-on sideburns.

"You look funny, Mommy," I said, my seven-year-old eyes looking up at my mother in awe.

When I'd come home crying about not having a father for the father-daughter dance, my mother had done what she always did, sprang into action to make me happy.

"My baby won't be fatherless at this dance," she'd announced as she headed toward the door. "Stay here. I'll be back in a few."

I knew everybody wouldn't have a daddy at the dance. But those that didn't have daddies would have uncles, or big brothers. But I didn't have anyone.

It had been just the two of us—Mommy and me—for as long as I could remember. Mama didn't even have boyfriends. Because at this point, I would have even taken a perfect stranger to the dance. I'd even told Mama that when she announced, "I have an idea," and went digging in the Halloween costume box for the mustache and sideburns.

Thirty minutes later, Mama had returned from Goodwill, wearing the man's suit coat, pants, and a hat. She didn't fool me though.

"Mommy, everybody can tell you're still a mommy," I giggled.

"You guys are second graders, nobody will know," she said, then she deepened her voice. "See, nobody can tell. I sound just like a man."

That made me burst out laughing because Mama did sound like a man with that deep hoarse voice.

"So we're going to go to the father-daughter dance and we're going to have a ball and it's going to just be our secret," she said.

"But what about your hair, Mommy?" I asked, as I studied her.

"Got that covered, too." She swooped up her long, stringy brown hair, tied it in a bun, put one of those wig cap things on her head and then slid the big brown hat back on her head. "The icing on the cake," Mama said.

I wanted to protest, but I couldn't. "Mommy, do you really think this will work?" I asked her.

"It will. I know it will," Mama replied. "And what's going to be great is that only you and I will know." She picked me up and swung me around and we both squealed in delight.

I don't know why that memory of the father-daughter dance remained so vivid in my mind. My mother was always doing thoughtful things like that to make up for all that I was missing in life. She'd always been there for me, always worked so that I didn't "feel" all that I was physically lacking.

Now, sitting here in this cold hospital room, watching her, I knew I would always be here for her. Thankfully, my mother hadn't suffered any major injuries from the fall down the steps, but because she'd been so disoriented, they immediately admitted her.

I replayed the reception fiasco over and over. I was sure Malcolm's family was super pissed at me. I thought about what my mother's doctor had told us on our last visit.

"Your mother may get aggressive, but know it's usually triggered by something—physical discomfort, environmental factors such as being in an unfamiliar situation, or even poor communication."

I shouldn't have made her wear that dress. I shouldn't have made her come.

I tried not to blame myself. The doctor had also told me not to take her actions to heart. That when she was in a "state," it was important to remember that this is not the same woman who raised me.

I leaned my head back against the seat in the hospital room at Ben Taub and pulled out my cell phone. I swiped until I got to Kendra's name and then pressed dial. The phone rang and rang. By now, the reception should have been wrapped up. Maybe Kendra and Travis were enjoying their honeymoon night. Hopefully, they'd been able to salvage the disaster my mother had created.

I ended the call and then did something I'd been dreading all evening, called my husband. For a minute, I didn't think he was going to answer.

"Hi, sweetheart," I said once he picked up.

"Hi," he replied, his tone dry. "How's your mother?" I knew that Malcolm loved my mother. But I could also tell there were days when he was thinking, "This isn't what I signed up for." He'd told me as much during one of our heated arguments. He later apologized and said he didn't mean it, but I knew there was some truth behind his words.

"She's asleep. Thankfully, she didn't break anything and will be okay. The doctor said she might have a slight concussion, but other than that, she'll be fine," I said. "Waiting on the doctor to come back with some more test results. They are keeping her overnight. How's Kendra?"

I heard a sharp inhale and then Malcolm said, "She's fine. She managed to pull it together and enjoy the rest of the reception. Travis's mother, on the other hand, not so much."

I paused, waiting on my husband to berate me with a barrage of "I told you sos."

"I'm so sorry," I said, when he didn't say anything. "I really—"

"Now's not the time," Malcolm said, cutting me off.

Now might not be the time, but I knew beyond a shadow of a doubt, the time was coming. Malcolm had tried to be supportive as my mother deteriorated. But he'd said we were now putting our lives on hold as my mother spiraled more and more out of control.

In the beginning, Mama had been staying with Aunt Marilyn, who was actually my great aunt, and her aunt. But Aunt Marilyn could no longer handle my mother, and she had become our problem. Malcolm had wanted to put her in a home but as frustrated as I got, I would never see my mother as a "problem," and it would break both of our hearts for me to put her in a home— not to mention, since we had no money, it would be one of the state-run facilities and I would die before I ever did something like that.

"Well, I don't suppose you'll make it for their breakfast in the morning?" Malcolm said.

I fought back the sadness that had been trying to overtake me all evening. Since I wasn't in the wedding, I had volunteered to host the breakfast for Kendra and Travis to open gifts.

"I doubt I'll make it," I said. "It really depends on how Mama is doing."

"She's in the hospital. Someone will be watching her," he snapped. "You can take a couple of hours to come to my sister's brunch, you know the thing that you are supposed to be hosting.

They're opening the gifts before they leave for the cruise and this was all your idea."

"I know Malcolm, but—"

He cut me off. "You know what? Do whatever you feel. Hope your mother gets better. I'll talk to you later." And he hung the phone up before I could say another word. It was unlike Malcolm to snap at me like that. My mother's situation was taking a toll on us all. I was just about to call my husband back when the doctor walked into the hospital room.

"Mrs. Reed?" he said.

I nodded. "Yes. Did you get the test results back?"

He took a deep breath and nodded. "Yes, and like I said earlier, everything is fine. Your mother is one lucky woman. She could have really done some damage."

"I know." Relief flooded me. My mother couldn't stand any more health issues.

Dr. Martin had been the doctor from her church who first diagnosed her. He'd stepped in after all the free clinics kept telling us nothing was wrong. He'd been treating my mother for the past six months and he had sided with Malcolm in saying that she should go into a home. I could tell by the concerned expression on his face that he believed that now more than ever.

"At some point you're going to have to reconsider her placement, Jill," Dr. Martin continued. "For her own good."

"But I thought you said the medication would help her get better?"

"I said it *may,* and unfortunately your mother seems to be one of those cases where the dementia is progressing much faster than we ever imagined."

That brought tears to my eyes.

His expression turned grim. "Jill, I have to warn you. I did a CAT scan of your mother's brain, and it's getting worse. You can expect more bad days than good ones, so . . ."

He let his words trail off and I nodded in understanding. I took a deep breath and took my mother's hand. "And I'll be right there through the good, the bad, and the ugly."

He nodded his understanding. "Your mother really is blessed to have a daughter like you."

I squeezed her hand. No, I was the one who'd been blessed with a mother like this.

Chapter 7

This was a rare occurrence—all of us sitting around our small kitchen table, enjoying a home-cooked meal. It had been a week since Kendra's wedding. My mother had only spent two nights in the hospital and now she was home, on new meds, and doing better than ever.

In fact, today, she had been quite lucid, and insisted on making collard greens, macaroni and cheese, black-eyed peas, and fried chicken. Of course, I stayed in the kitchen with her the whole time, but it had been one of those "like old times moments," where we laughed and joked about any and everything. Even Malcolm had gotten in on the joy. He had gotten a promising job interview today, so he was in a good mood. Though he said removing the stress of how to pay bills would allow him to focus on his app development.

"Dinner's ready," my mother sang as she walked over to the kitchen table carrying a bowl of macaroni and cheese.

Malcolm made sure Destiny was settled in her highchair and then we sat down and began to make small talk as we ate.

"So, tell me about your job interview. Why do you think you're going to get this one?" I said as I bit into a piece of fried chicken. I closed my eyes and savored the taste. Just like old times.

"I don't know. I just got a good feeling about this one," Malcolm replied. "I'm overqualified, but I could tell that the guy I interviewed with really liked me. I'd be working on the city's fleet. I was able to show him something that had been wrong with one of the city vehicles the whole time. So needless to say, he was excited because they hadn't been able to figure out what was wrong with the engine, and I fixed it just like that." Malcolm snapped his fingers. His enthusiasm made me proud. Too bad maintenance was something he did on the side, because he really was good at fixing things.

"Well, I sure hope so, baby," I said. I reached over and handed Destiny a piece of mashed up cornbread.

"Yeah, baby. This is what we need," Malcolm continued. "This job would give me like a fifteen-thousand-dollar raise over what I was making before I was laid off. If we keep living off my original salary, we could put that extra aside to save so I can finish the app. I think I've worked out the kinks."

My mother smiled as she sipped her sweet tea. "Well, you shouldn't have to worry about money," she said.

Both Malcolm and I looked at her and managed a smile. "Yeah, don't we wish? We always worry about money," Malcolm said.

"No. Jill's rich."

"You're so right. I'm rich in love, Mother," I replied, patting her hand.

"You're rich in money, too," she said with a sheepish grin.

"Tell that to our bank account." Malcolm and I laughed at the same time.

"Your dad has a lot of money. I don't know where he is, but you really should call him. He'll help. He'll help you pay some bills." She nodded matter-of-factly as she popped a spoonful of macaroni and cheese into her mouth.

Her serious tone made me lose my smile. "Mom . . ."

Malcolm narrowed his eyes at me and then a wide smile covered his face and he winked at me.

"Ms. Connie, how can we find this rich daddy of Jill's?"

I cut my eyes at my husband; I really didn't like when he entertained my mother's delusions.

"I told you, I don't know how to get in touch with him anymore, but he has a lot of money. All your money problems would be solved if you just asked him." Mama shrugged.

"All our problems will be solved?" Malcolm said, feigning excitement. "Well Jill, you better call him right now. Let me guess. Her daddy is Denzel James Earl Jones."

Mama shook her head. "No, silly. Those are celebrities. And two different people."

"Oh." Malcolm shrugged and suppressed a giggle.

"But Jill's daddy is just as rich as them," Mama continued. "Probably richer."

I put my hand over my mother's and kept my voice calm as I said, "Mama, my daddy died a long time ago."

The smile left her face and she frowned like she was trying to reach back into the recesses of her mind. "He did? How do you know?"

"Because you told me. We grew up without him. He died when I was a baby, remember?"

She looked extremely confused as she scratched the side of her head. "He's dead? What did his wife say? Is she heartbroken?"

"You were his wife, Mama."

Her eyebrows scrunched together, she frowned, and a mist covered her eyes. "I didn't mean to kill him."

Now I knew she was gone. Which meant our moment of family joy was gone as well.

"I am so sorry," my mother said as tears started running down her face. "I didn't mean to kill him," she repeated.

Malcolm stopped smiling as a look of trepidation passed across his face. "It's okay, Ms. Connie. I wasn't trying to upset you."

"I didn't mean to," she said, shaking her head. "I am really so sorry."

"Mama, let me help you go lie down." I said, pushing back from the table and easing over to help her up.

She was in full-fledged crying mode now and the outburst startled Destiny, who started crying, too. "I'm so, so sorry," she continued.

"Why don't you just go lie down?" I repeated.

"I have to clean the kitchen and get ready for the funeral," she said.

I debated trying to convince her that there was no funeral, but I remembered how Dr. Martin said it was fruitless to argue with a dementia patient. Instead, I just said, "Malcolm and I will do the dishes."

"Okay," she sniffed.

She let me lead her upstairs to her bedroom, where I got her settled, once again. I returned to the kitchen just as Malcolm was clearing the table.

"I'm getting really worried about Mama," I said. "The rambling and delusion is getting progressively worse."

Malcolm stopped setting a dish in the sink and then turned around and looked at me. The expression on his face was hard to make out. "How much do you really know about your father?" he asked.

"What?" I replied, tilting my head as if that would help me understand his question better. "What kind of question is that?"

"I don't know." He shrugged. "Yeah, I think your mom is rambling, but sometimes I feel like there may be something to what she's saying. I know it's easy to dismiss it, but something about the conviction in her voice makes me think that this isn't delusional rambling."

I shook my head as I walked over to finish clearing the table. "Okay, now you're starting to sound crazy like her."

He shrugged as he continued to help me. "I'm just saying. You might want to want to consider that there may be more to what she's talking about."

"My mother is delusional. Dementia comes and goes." I blew an exasperated breath and snatched the plates of food to box up for lunch tomorrow.

"Look, I didn't mean you'd get you upset," he said, when he noticed me slamming stuff. "I just thought maybe it's something you might want to look into because that's not the first time she has said that."

"All I need to look into is getting my mom some help and hoping that we can find some type of care," I huffed.

"Okay." Malcolm leaned in and kissed me on the forehead, instantly causing some of my irritation to dissipate. My husband's touch always did that to me. "Don't be mad at me, babe," he said. "I was just bringing up a suggestion."

"Well, it's a dumb suggestion."

He threw his hands up in surrender. "If you say so."

"I say so," I said, as I started running the dishwater, signaling an end to this conversation. I'd spent my whole life yearning for my father. I wasn't even going to entertain the idea that he could possibly be alive.

Chapter 8

Today was going to be crazy. I could tell by the line that was out the door when I arrived at work. Our location was in a prime spot near the Galleria Mall, so we stayed busy. While I was grateful for my job, I would never understand how people paid five dollars for a cup of coffee every day, sometimes two and three times a day. I smiled at Tony because I was five minutes early and he just shook his head as he scrambled to fill an order. I don't know what Mr. Logan had said to him, but I showed up the next day at work and Tony never mentioned my outburst again, so naturally, neither did I.

I took my place at the register and helped move the line along. I wasn't put on this earth to be a Starbucks barista, but I was good at my job and it was paying the bills until I could get back on my feet.

I had just wrapped up a large order when I looked up to see the man from the other day. "Good afternoon, Mr. Logan," I said as he approached my register.

"Remember, I asked you to call me Major," he replied.

My mother had taught me to always show my elders respect by greeting them as Mr. and Mrs. So I wouldn't be honoring his request, but I simply smiled. "Will you be having your usual tall, no-water chai?"

"Yes," he said, fidgeting. He appeared nervous as he turned to glance back at a man who stood in back of him in what looked like a very expensive, tailored suit. The man nodded like he was encouraging Mr. Logan, who then turned back to me. "So, what time do you get off? Are you taking a break today?"

I hesitated. I hoped he didn't think I was going to get back in the car with him, especially if his creepy wife was in there.

"I'm uh, actually I'm about to go on break in about thirty minutes. Why do you want to know?"

"Well, I would like to talk to you."

"About what?" I asked. I wasn't just going to follow him all willy-nilly this time.

"It's . . . it's very important," he replied. He glanced around, leaned in and added, "And private. Do you mind if I just sit over here and enjoy my tea until you go on your break? I promise I won't take up much of your time."

I shrugged, really wondering what this was all about. I knew the only way I would find out what he wanted was to talk to him. I was going to get some answers from Mr. Logan today or he could hang up the creepy meetings.

Thirty-five minutes later I went on my break and Mr. Logan was waiting patiently just like he'd said he would be. Now my curiosity was definitely piqued. I walked over to the corner table, where he was now sitting with the man in the tailored suit.

"So, what's going on?" I asked as I slid into the chair. I tried to act nonchalant but I was dying to know this man's end game.

Mr. Logan inhaled, like he was summoning up his strength. His manicured nails and well-groomed black and silver beard showed that he was a man of confidence and didn't seem like the type who was easily rattled, so why he was acting nervous was beyond me.

After taking another deep breath, Mr. Logan began. "Well, as you know, I've been coming in here quite regularly for the last few months."

I nodded but didn't reply. I didn't want to interrupt anything he was about to say.

"Someone else actually first told me about you and so I came to see for myself," he continued.

Now my eyebrows rose and my eyes narrowed. Why would anybody be telling him about me? But I remained quiet as he continued. He nodded toward the man that was sitting across from him and the man took out a Manila envelope. Mr. Logan opened it and removed what looked like an eight-by-ten baby photo.

"In 1993, my daughter, Alicia, was kidnapped," Mr. Logan said, as the other man slid the photo toward me.

I glanced at the picture of the fair-skinned baby with bright eyes and big dimples. Her curls peeked from under a white, ruffled hat. And she had on a long white dress that looked like it cost more than the most expensive thing in my closet. I looked up at Mr. Logan again but this time I said, "I'm sorry to hear about your daughter."

The man in the suit pulled out another picture. Mr. Logan took that one, glanced at it, then slid it toward me.

"This is an age rendition photo." He pointed to the first picture. "That was Alicia a month after she was born. A week before she was kidnapped." He tapped the second picture. "This is what we believe she looks like, aged to her twenty-seven years."

I took the picture that looked like it had been drawn by a sketch artist and held it up. From the tiny nose, the dimple on the right side, to the light brown naturally curly hair and deep hazel eyes . . . "Th-this looks like me," I said in confusion.

A knowing smile spread across Mr. Logan's face. "It does, doesn't it? We've been circulating that photo for years. My friend who happened to see you working here knew about this picture and he told me about you."

I shook my head trying to make sense of this. "Wait," I finally said as it dawned on me what he was trying to say. "You think I'm your missing daughter?"

He slowly nodded. I couldn't help it, I burst out laughing. The kind of laughter that starts in your belly and moves up into your chest and out of your mouth. "I'm sorry," I said when I noticed I was the only one laughing. "I don't mean to make light of the tragedy that you had in your life but trust me, I'm not your daughter." I slid both pictures back toward him. "I may look like this picture that an artist drew, but that's not me. No one kidnapped me. I've never been missing. But I do hope that you find your daughter."

"We think that he already has," the other man said, finally speaking.

I studied both of them for a moment, waiting for someone to burst out with an "April Fool's" even though it was September.

"Look, I don't know what kind of game y'all trying to run," I said, getting a little irritated when I saw they were really serious, "but I'm the daughter of Connie and Al Harrison."

The man was about to say something, but Mr. Logan held his hand up before he could get his words out.

"I understand that you were *raised* by Connie Harrison, though I've never heard of this Al Harrison," Mr. Logan said.

"Well, I don't mean to be rude, but I don't really care who you've heard of. I was raised by Connie, my mother. My father, Al, died when I was a baby."

He exchanged more knowing looks with the man. Then, he looked back at me and leaned in on the table, his gaze meeting me head-on. "Well, the thing is, we believe you *are* our daughter, stolen from us when you were just a baby. And we would like to have you take a DNA test just to confirm our suspicion, though my wife is convinced beyond a shadow of a doubt—you know, that whole mother's intuition thing."

"Well, your wife doesn't know what she's talking about." Now I was insulted. And pissed that I'd given these whack jobs any of my precious break time. "I don't know if this is some kind of cult ring you're trying to get me hooked up in, but I know who I belong to, and this foolishness that you're talking to me about is just that, foolishness." I stood. "Now I'm sorry you've been wasting your time coming to check me out, but I can assure you that I'm not your daughter."

I turned to leave and Mr. Logan jumped up and grabbed my arm. "Wait," he said, taking my hand.

I glared at his arm gripping mine and he instantly released his grip.

"Please?" he nodded and the man slid the envelope back to me. "Take the pictures. My information is in there. Just review everything and then come meet with us. Or better yet, ask your mother about it and see what she has to say."

I wanted to tell him there was no way in hell I would take this nonsense back to my mother, but instead I figured the sooner I could get away from him, the better off I'd be. "Okay, fine," I said, taking the envelope.

"Please, seriously, look at this," he repeated. "And I'll be in touch."

"Don't bother," I replied as I tucked the envelope under my arm. "Now, if you'll excuse me, I'd like to go enjoy what's left of my break."

I left without giving them a chance to reply. I headed to the break room, fighting the urge to toss the envelope with the photos into the trash. I knew I should've tossed them, but the little girl in the photo had me intrigued. Not because I really thought she was me, I knew better. But the tiny, clover-looking birthmark on her arm had me shook. Because it was just like mine.

Chapter 9

Out of all the crazy, cockamamie theories I'd heard in my life, this one took the cake. I don't know what kind of scam or con game this Major Logan was running, but he was on some kind of potent drug if he thought I was going to be gullible enough to fall for his claim. My mother had pictures of her being pregnant. She had been there my whole life. If I had been kidnapped . . . well, the very idea was ludicrous.

But why in the world would they be targeting me? It's not like I had anything to offer.

I dialed Malcolm's cellphone. He didn't answer so I left a message.

"Babe, you're not going to believe this." Before I could finish, his number came through on the other line. I didn't finish my message as I clicked over.

"Hey, bae," he said. "Sorry I didn't get to the phone in time. I was in the zone. I think I've figured out the semantics that kept giving me an error on this app design." I could hear the excitement in his voice. "What's up?"

"I'm leaving work," I said, grateful that he didn't go off on a tangent about his app.

"Why do you sound upset?" he asked.

"Because I am upset, frustrated, exasperated, along with everything else." I huffed. "You remember the guy I told you that came by Starbucks acting all weird with his wife?"

"Yeah, what about him?" The excitement that filled his voice just moments ago shifted to full-on protective mode.

"Well, he showed back up today and you will not believe what he said."

"What?" Malcolm asked. His voice was tense now as if he was preparing to defend his woman.

"He said that he believed I was his daughter who had been kidnapped at birth." The words sounded crazy even coming out of my mouth.

Silence momentarily filled the phone. Then he said, "What?"

"He thinks I'm his long lost daughter," I replied. "Isn't that the craziest thing you've ever heard?" I wanted to tell him about the matching birthmark, but I'd chalked that up to coincidence so there was no need to even bring that up.

"Just because they have this age rendition photo that looks like me, they've gotten it into their head that I'm their daughter. That I was stolen when I was just a few weeks old . . ."

"What? They think you were kidnapped? Who is this dude?"

"I don't know. I mean he seemed legitimate—the designer suit, luxury car, everything seemed legit—until he opened his mouth talking about some kidnapping," I said.

Malcolm was quiet for a minute, like he was really thinking. Then he said, "You don't think that's really possible, do you?"

"Of course I don't. That's crazy." I jumped at the sound of the driver blaring his horn as I tried to get over. I was so discombobulated that I didn't even see him.

"Who does he think kidnapped you?" Malcolm asked, pulling me back into the conversation. "How did someone kidnap you? Why would someone take you?"

Malcolm was asking questions I had no idea how to answer, and I don't know why, but it was extremely irritating. "Well, he never got to that part. But the very idea that my mother kidnapped me is just dumb because not only do I know my mother, I saw pictures of her when she was pregnant. I have so many ways just like my mother. I am my mother's child."

Silence filled the phone again until my husband said, "Wow. This is crazy. You know who you should ask about this, though? Your Aunt Marilyn," Malcolm added.

"I don't need to ask anybody about anything," I snapped.

"Hey, don't get testy with me," he said. "I'm just trying to help you make sense of it."

"Yeah, well, there is nothing to make sense of, because the very idea is ludicrous." The fact that Malcolm hadn't immediately jumped on my 'this is asinine' bandwagon had aggravated me, so I was ready to get off the phone. "I don't even want to talk about this anymore. I'm going to get my *mother*," I said, stressing her title. "And we'll be home in a little bit."

I hung up the phone and continued making my way to the adult day care facility, and then at the last minute, I decided to turn right instead of going left down the road that took me to the facility. Maybe Malcolm was right and Aunt Marilyn could help me figure out what Mr. Logan's game was.

Ten minutes later I was pulling up in front of my aunt's dilapidated home. She had a son who was a doctor in Louisiana and he tried on multiple occasions to fix her home up but she was content with it just like it was.

"Hey, baby girl," Aunt Marilyn said when she saw me walking in her kitchen, "you're just in time to help me shell peas."

"Aunt Marilyn, nobody shells peas anymore," I said, chuckling as I took a seat at the table across from her.

"You do," she said, sliding the bowl toward me.

I chuckled as I picked up the vegetable and began cracking it open. "Why don't you just buy your peas already shelled?" I asked, dropping the peas into a bowl the way she'd taught me when I was a little girl.

"Because they come with pesticides and all other kind of stuff that I don't want in my body. Besides, fresh is always better." She snapped a pea and tossed it into the ceramic bowl. "So what brings you over here?"

I wrestled with how to say what was on my mind. "Well, I have some things I'd like to talk to you about."

"Talk away," she said, then nodded toward my hands, that had paused shelling, "but shell as you talk."

I laughed as I picked up another pea. "So, you basically raised Mama after her parents died, right?" I snapped a pea, then tossed it in the bowl as I tried to gauge her reaction.

Aunt Marilyn nodded. "Yes, but you know this already."

"So, can you tell me a little bit about when she found out she was pregnant with me?" I asked.

Aunt Marilyn shrugged and said, "You know my memory is bad. I can't remember all of that."

"Aunt Marilyn, please?"

She titled her head like she was studying me. "What you want to know, baby?"

What *did* I want to know? 'There isn't any chance that I was stolen, is there?' just didn't seem like the right question to ask my elderly aunt.

"I want to know how old Mama was when she had me. And did you ever meet my daddy? Just anything you can tell me," I said, suddenly realizing how desperate I was for Aunt Marilyn to shed some light on the crazy that had waltzed into my life the past few hours.

She paused like she was thinking, then she said, "Well, your mama went away to school."

"At Wiley College in Marshall, right?"

"Yeah. Too bad she didn't finish," Aunt Marilyn tsked.

"So, my daddy was a student there?"

"I believe so," Aunt Marilyn said. "She was so in love with that boy. Always writing home about him. I wanted her to focus on her studies and not some boy."

"Did you ever meet him?"

Aunt Marilyn shook her head. "No. I think that was part of my issue with him. Marshall is only three hours away and I felt like if he couldn't make time to come meet her people, how great could he really be. But you couldn't say that to your mama. She loved that man something fierce. After her first year, I assumed they'd broken up, because your mama kind of disappeared."

I frowned. "Disappeared? What does that mean?"

"It means she disappeared. She came home right when school was out and she was so sad, would barely get out of bed. Spent the whole summer moping, talking about she was sick. And when I tried to talk about your daddy, she would just burst into tears. I knew those tears. Those were heartbroken tears."

"They must've gotten back together, then?" I said.

Aunt Marilyn looked like she was thinking. Then she replied, "Well, obviously, because here you are."

"When did Mama snap out of her sadness?" I asked.

"Toward the end of the summer. She finally got up out that bed and was always gone in the streets. Like I said, she would just disappear. Oh, I fussed but she was grown and I didn't have the energy to keep up with her. Besides, I was just happy she wasn't so sad and moping anymore. Then one day, about three weeks before school was supposed to start back up, she announced that she was going back to school." Aunt Marilyn stood and walked over to the stove. "You want some tea, sugar?"

I just wanted her to finish this story. I don't know why I'd never heard it.

"No thank you," I replied. "So she got back with Daddy when she went back to school?"

My aunt lit a match, put it to the gas stove and waited for the flame to flicker on. Then she filled the teapot with water and set it on the fire.

"Yeah, I'm guessing so," she said once the water was heating up. "Because next thing I know, she come talking about she's with child. Near 'bout broke my heart. I felt like I'd let her mama down by letting her get pregnant out of wedlock."

"But you saw her when she was pregnant, right?"

Aunt Marilyn frowned like she didn't understand the question. "Jillian, why are you asking me all of this? What's going on?" she said, putting her hands on her round hips.

"I just want to know," I said.

She folded her arms across her chest like she didn't believe me. "Of course I saw her when she was pregnant." She hesitated and her eyes went to the top of her head like she was trying to recall. "I mean, I think I did. But don't you have a picture at home of when she was pregnant?"

"Yes," I said, fondly remembering how much my mother loved that picture of her standing in front of Greater Sweet Home Baptist Church in Marshall. She was only about seven-months pregnant, but you could tell how happy she was.

"I was really upset when your mama turned up pregnant," Aunt Marilyn continued. "But she was determined to give you the best life."

"And she tried," I said.

"Yes. Yes, she did." That brought a smile to Aunt Marilyn's face.

"Another question," I said, knowing my time was limited. I knew my great-aunt. I only had a few more questions before she'd shut this conversation down completely. "So has anyone ever met my father?"

"No. You know we didn't have a lot of money, so there wasn't a whole bunch of traveling back and forth. Shoot, by the time we found out she was pregnant, she was almost due. Then when she moved home when you were about three months old, she said she and your daddy were no longer together."

That gave me a bit of relief. If my mother was pregnant, then showed up with me a few months later, the timeline would make perfect sense. "So were they together when he died?"

Aunt Marilyn shrugged. "Your mama didn't talk about your daddy much after that."

"So, I was born in Marshall or here?"

"Well, you was born there because your mama was going to try and finish school but she couldn't do both."

"This isn't making any sense. I thought I was born here in Houston," I said, finding it strange that Mama would go into childbirth and not a single friend or family member was there with her.

"You know what? I'm getting confused. I'm not sure. I'm too old to remember this stuff." She walked back over to the sink.

"Aunt Marilyn, this is important," I said.

"Why?" She turned to me. "Why do you need to know all this now?"

I debated telling her about Major Logan and then decided against it. It wouldn't do anything but upset her as well, and I knew the man was lying.

"No reason. I just was asking," I said, releasing a heavy sigh. I was getting worked up for nothing. Things might not add up but if it was one thing that I was sure of—it was that I was Connie Harrison's daughter.

Chapter 10

Today was a good day. My mother had Destiny cradled in her arms as they sat and watched *The Princess and the Frog* on TV. I didn't know if my daughter even understood what was happening, but she was just as enamored with Princess Tiana as my mother, and watching the two of them brought a smile to my face. I was sitting at the kitchen table going through my laptop, looking for online schools, trying to see if there would be any way I could afford to go back in and finish my degree.

We had just about wrapped up the movie when I heard the key in the door turn. Malcolm walked in and I could tell from the look on his face something was wrong. Destiny had fallen asleep and my mother was now watching something on HGTV.

"Hey, y'all," Malcolm mumbled as he tossed his keys on the bar.

"Hi, Malcolm," my mother said and smiled. Her smile instantly brightened his mood.

He leaned down and kissed Destiny on the forehead, then asked my mother, "How are you feeling today?" His voice was filled with genuine concern.

"I'm good," she replied. "Today has been a good day."

He looked to me for confirmation and I nodded. "It really has." I smiled at my mother. "They've been watching movies and

I think we're going to have to get your daughter a Princess Tiana doll because she is in love."

He nodded, but I could tell by the look on his face, he was distracted. Finally, he said, "Mama Connie, do you mind going and taking Destiny to your room to lie down? I need to talk to Jill for a minute."

"Of course," my mother said. "She fell asleep during the movie. Jill didn't think she'd understand it, but she just loved it."

"That's good," he replied.

My mother eased up, careful not to wake the baby, and headed up the stairs to her bedroom. My first instinct was to follow her, but since it had been a good day, I figured everything would be fine.

"What's going on?" I asked after they were out of earshot. I had hoped that it was news that he had gotten a job but his expression was troubled, so that couldn't be it.

"Let's go out on the patio so I can talk to you," he whispered. Now my interest was really piqued.

"Okay." I followed him, my nerves revving up because of the expression on his face and his tense demeanor.

Malcolm eased the patio door closed.

"Okay, what's going on, Malcolm?" I asked him.

He sighed, then motioned for me to take a seat. "Please sit," he said once I didn't move.

"I'm good," I said, waving his request off. "Just tell me what's going on."

Malcolm had a habit of fidgeting whenever he didn't know how to tell me something. Finally, he said, "Well, you know you told me about the Starbucks guy, right?"

I rolled my eyes. "Is this what this is about? Let me guess, you googled and saw the whole story about the baby being kidnapped? Yeah, I saw it, too."

"So, you did look it up?" he asked.

I nodded. For some reason, the story was intriguing to me. Not because I believed it, but because I could only imagine what it had to be like for a family to have their child kidnapped.

"Yes, I did look it up, and none of it adds up to me being that missing baby. I think because the time frame was around the same time, Mr. Logan and his wife are drawing these crazy conclusions. I was born in Marshall, Texas, when my mom was at Wiley College. This kidnapping happened in Beaumont. I don't even know why the two would add up. Plus, how would my mother even know a family like the Logans?"

Malcolm's eyes shifted down to his lap as he took a seat in one of our five-dollar lawn chairs—another steal from Goodwill. "Well, there are a lot of things that don't add up," he said. "Including some details surrounding your birth."

"What is that supposed to mean?" I asked. "My birth certificate shows I was born to Connie and Al Harrison."

"But doesn't your birth certificate say you were born in Houston?"

I hesitated, not wanting to deal with that piece of information. "Yes," I finally replied.

"So why do you now say you were born in Marshall?" he asked.

"Because that's what Aunt Marilyn told me. But I'm sure it's all a mix-up."

"That's just it," he sighed. "I knew that things didn't add up. Between some of the stuff your mom says—"

"My mother suffers from dementia," I said, cutting him off. "You cannot put a lot of stake into the things she says."

"Yes, but some of the things she has said, she's so sure about. We blow them off as the crazy talking. But I've been reading up, sometimes people suffering from dementia have trouble remembering lies."

"So you're calling my mother a liar?" I asked.

He held his hand up. "No, it's not that," he protested, then released another heavy sigh. "It's this." He pulled an envelope out of his jacket.

"What is that?" I asked.

"You know my cousin Francesca works at the Social Security office?"

I raised an eyebrow. "Yes, I know that," I said, my words measured.

"Well, I had her pull your birth certificate."

"You did what?" I screamed. "Why would you do that?"

"Because this isn't adding up, and a wealthy man doesn't come out of the blue trying to claim you as his child unless he really believes you're his child."

"This is ridiculous," I said, stomping across the room. "You do know that, right?"

"I don't know anything, except . . ." he paused, carefully weighing his next words. "Your birth certificate is a fake."

I stopped my trek across our bedroom. "What?"

He handed me the paper. "There is no record of your birth."

"Huh? There must be some kind of mistake," I said, snatching the paper and quickly scanning it. It was an email from Francesca. Simple words that bore insurmountable weight:

Malcolm,
This birth certificate is fraudulent. It's doesn't even have the right seal on it. I checked all the databases in Texas and there is no record of a Jillian Harrison ever being born and the social security number belongs to a woman who died in 1961.

I glanced up at my husband. His face now mirrored mine—screaming the question what in the world was really going on?

Chapter 11

The picture glared at me. Almost as if it were taunting me. Almost as if it wanted to say, "You know I'm you."

I fought back the lump in my throat as I fingered my computer screen like I could really feel the baby's soft butterscotch skin. The headline blared: "Family desperate for answers."

I reread the article that I could've had memorized by now.

Major and Elaine Logan plead for the kidnapper to return their child. The baby was kidnapped from an area park by a woman witnesses describe as an older black woman with a small gray afro, though authorities now believe the woman was wearing a disguise.

And as I'd done the last ten times I'd read the article, I stopped reading at the photo. Major Logan stood stoically, his face reeking of pain. But it was the face of the woman next to him that made my stomach turn. The face of the woman from the car. Her light brown hair that matched mine, her hazel eyes. Her white skin.

All my life, I had questioned my light skin next to my mother's bronze complexion. But my mother had always made me feel at ease by telling me my father was from New Orleans, so I was part Creole. There was another girl who was Creole who lived on our street, and since our skin was the same color, that explanation had worked for me.

Could it be? Could I be part white, not part Creole?

No. I shook away that thought.

"There still has to be another explanation," I mumbled. But there was no arguing the birth certificate. Why would my mother have faked my birth certificate? *How* would she have faked my birth certificate. And my social security number?

Malcolm knew that I was having a hard time processing everything. He'd left me alone with my thoughts and had gone to watch TV. And when I'd stomped through the living room, into the kitchen, grabbed a bottled water and stomped upstairs to our bedroom, he didn't say a word.

I did momentarily ask myself why I was angry with my husband. Because he'd gone digging, trying to help me find answers? Or because I didn't like what he had unearthed?

Later, Malcolm brought Destiny into our room, put her in her crib, then climbed in bed next to me and just held me. That was the beauty of our relationship. No matter how mad I got at him, he had a way of touching my soul. And for a moment, I was able to put aside the upheaval of my life and seek comfort in my husband's touch.

Malcolm caressed my arm, and though my mind wanted to protest, my body welcomed his touch. I kept my back to him, though I did scoot back and snuggle a little closer. His caressing gave way to kissing and the silence became our aphrodisiac. He took his time, his mouth moving from my arm to the arch of my back. My heart was beating a New York marathon—all these years later and Malcolm could still make my heart race.

"Baby," I said, turning over to face him. "I'm sure—"

His lips punctuated his silent rebuke. He moved his tongue along the wisps of my hairline, over to my ear. I savored the fact that no matter how bad things got on the outside, on the inside, when it was just the two of us, struggling to keep quiet so we didn't wake our daughter, Malcolm and I could get lost in each other. He was unerringly gentle, caressing me like I was the painting to his Picasso. Every stroke reminded me why I loved this man. And there, in our full-sized bed, Malcolm took me back to the night of our honeymoon, when we made love, talked about our big dreams that lay ahead, then made love again.

The closeness that I felt as we exploded together then collapsed into each other's arms gave me faith that this storm I was in would pass.

When the morning sun peeked in through our blinds, I eased from under Malcolm's arm and slid out of the bed. It was back to reality, and back to my laptop, and the news article.

I read for another ten minutes, then decided to go for a run to try and clear my head. I wasn't getting any answers just re-reading the same thing over and over.

On my forty-five-minute trek, I came to the conclusion that the only way I would get any answers was straight from the source, which is why after returning home and getting Destiny fed and settled, I'd awakened my mother and told her to get dressed so we could go out.

"I'm ready," my mother said, appearing in the doorway.

I took in the sight of the woman I had loved since birth. When I was little, my mother used to dress me and her up in matching outfits and we had a regular date. Mother-daughter time was important to my mother and she made sure at least twice a month, we got our uninterrupted time to go do something special. Movies when she could afford it. Walks in the park when she couldn't. I remembered many days when Mama would be called in for work at the hospital and she would tell them, "I can't do it today. It's Jill's time."

That had always made me feel special. Even though we needed the money, my mother would never budge when it came to her "Jill time."

A slow tear trickled down my cheek as I thought about all the struggles we had endured in our lives. I was seven years old before I even realized that we were poor because of what my mother had given me. The love my mother showed me had been priceless.

"So where are we going?" my mother asked, not noticing my melancholy mood.

I took a deep breath, wiped away my budding tears, and stood. "We are going to have Mommy-Jill time."

"Really?" she said. "Oh my God. We haven't had that in years. Where's Destiny?"

"Malcolm is going to take her to Miss Betty," I said, referring to our sometimes-babysitter who lived two doors down. "I wanted to make sure that you and I had our uninterrupted time."

That made my mother squeal in delight. "Let's go then." She didn't even ask where we were going like she normally did. She was just happy to be going.

My mother and I had an amazing lunch, reminiscing about old times. Dementia had snatched her current memories, but her memories of the past remained intact. That's what I was banking on to get answers about my birth.

When they first brought out our meals, I could tell my mother was getting a little flustered when she tried to eat her food with her knife. But other than that, I felt like she was lucid enough for us to have a meaningful conversation.

"So Mom, I have something I want to talk with you about," I said, folding the napkin across my lap and struggling to find the words. "I know this is going to sound crazy." I inhaled again before continuing, "but this man showed up at my job and he said, he thought, well, he believes that . . . I may be his daughter."

My mother's eyes bucked. "You're . . . you're *my* d-daughter," she stammered.

"I know that," I said. I placed my hand over hers, trying to ease her nerves before she got worked up. "But, he thinks that I'm his. His daughter that was kidnapped."

"Kidnapped?" She was emphatic as she added, "No. No. I gave birth to you. You're my daughter."

And then she began reciting the story of my birth. One that I'd heard countless times. One that I could recite right along with her.

"Your dad was away in the military. Nobody was there with me as I toiled seventeen long hours to bring you into this world," she said. "I didn't use any drugs. I wanted everything to be as natural as possible. And so as much as it hurt, I endured it in order to bring you into the world the right way."

For the first time in all my years of hearing this story, I couldn't help but note how it sounded . . . rehearsed.

"Okay, Mom. I know. You've told me about how you carried me and how you were alone."

She slammed her palm on the table. "Exactly! I, *alone*, raised you."

"I know, Mom. Don't get worked up," I calmly replied.

She slumped back down in her seat. Her voice cracked as she said, "Why is he doing this?" she asked. "You're my daughter."

"I don't know why he would say something like that. That's what I'm trying to figure out," I replied.

She seemed to calm down. "You believe him?" she asked. Her voice was soft like she was dreading my answer.

I wanted to say "of course not," but after that fake birth certificate, I didn't know what to believe.

"Mom, the issue that I'm having is that I've found out my birth certificate is a fake," I gently said.

"Says who? That's crazy. You got a job. How would you have gotten a job if your birth certificate was a fake?"

I shrugged. "I don't know, especially because it appears that my social security number isn't real either."

"Ridiculous," she huffed. "You would've never been able to go to school or get a job with a fake birth certificate and social security number," she added. Her eyebrows had furrowed as if she was trying to get me to see that this was an absurd claim. "Someone at the birth certificate office made a mistake. Your birth is real."

Now she did have a point there, but still, there was so much that wasn't adding up.

My mother's anger gave way to tears as she fell back in her chair. "But if you want to be somebody else's daughter, fine."

"Mother. Stop," I said. Next thing I knew, she was sobbing uncontrollably. "Mom."

"You're going to leave me," she cried.

"I'm not leaving you," I said, scooting my chair closer to her to console her, especially before people around us started staring more than they already were. "Remember what you used to tell me when I was a little girl? Love never leaves. I'm here forever and always, okay? I'm sorry I brought it up."

She put her arms around my neck. "Please don't leave me, Jill. Please don't leave me," she wailed.

The waiter stopped at our table. "Is everything okay?"

I nodded and gave an apologetic shrug to the people in the restaurant who were staring at us. "Just—just give me a second, please?" I told the waiter. "My mother is upset about something."

He nodded and walked away.

"Mom, I need you to calm down. Look at me." I said, taking her chin and raising it toward me. "I'm not going anywhere. Okay? I just asked because he came to my job and asked me. You're my mother. I know that and no one can ever tell me otherwise."

That finally made her smile.

"And you're my daughter," she sniffed. "Nothing will ever change that."

I returned her smile. She was right. Whatever Major Logan and his family thought to be true, it was one thing that I knew—I was my mother's daughter and like she said, nothing would ever change that.

Chapter 12

"I hate to say this, but your mama's running game on you."

I cut my eyes at my friend Cynthia as she sat across from me in the beauty shop. We were in the waiting area of Serenity Hair Studio to get our hair done. Our beautician, Wanda, had already taken my mother back and now Cynthia and I were just sitting and talking. I'd just filled her in on my dilemma with the birth certificate and she'd cursed me out for not telling her earlier. Then, she went right into super snoop mode.

"Mama Connie is definitely sick, but she is also smart enough to know when to play the sick card."

"My mother wouldn't lie about something like this." I paused, before adding, "Would she?"

Cynthia shrugged. "I wouldn't have thought so, but now, I don't know. But really, what is your mama supposed to say, 'hey baby I kidnapped you from this man and this white woman when you were an infant, but it's all good because I love you?'" She took a sip of her bottled water. "And didn't you say this guy claiming to be your father is a multi-millionaire? Shoot, you'd better hope that he is your real daddy. If he's not, I'll be his daughter since I haven't seen my deadbeat dad since I was ten."

I knew Cynthia didn't mean anything by making light of this situation, but there was nothing funny or comical about what I was going through. If indeed what these people were saying, what all signs were pointing toward, was true, and I was not my mother's biological child, that would mean so many things. First and foremost, it would mean that my mother had lied to me my whole life. Secondly, it would mean that I didn't know a single thing about my real history. And third, the hardest, was that my mother was a criminal. It was all just too much to process. When I'd left lunch, I'd gone back to the idea that this whole thing was crazy. Then I'd met up with Cynthia at the beauty shop. I told her the story and now I was back to wondering if the allegations were true.

This roller coaster ride was killing me.

"What would you do in this situation?" I asked Cynthia.

"Girl, I would need to know. I would have to have some concrete answers," she said. "And I wouldn't be able to rest until I got them from someone other than your mother, because she's the one with the most to lose."

"So you don't think this whole thing is crazy?"

Cynthia leaned over to make sure no one was listening, then she whispered, "I did at first. But fake birth certificates, a fake social security number, a past that doesn't add up, and like Malcolm said, some of the things your mother says—it just makes this all questionable."

I think that's the part that had been bothering me the most. After Malcolm and I had made love the other night, he'd gone to sleep, but I'd lain awake replaying all the things my mother had said over the past few months that I'd chalked up to "crazy talk."

"Jill's daddy is just as rich as them."

"One day, your mother will come."

"They're going to be really mad. They're going to want you back."

"Plus," Cynthia continued, interrupting my thoughts, "rich dudes don't go around claiming kids that aren't theirs."

"So, what do I do?" I asked.

Cynthia leaned back in her chair.

"Go see these people, the Logans," she replied. "I mean, they could be your family. Find out one way or the other or else it will drive you crazy. You need to get some answers and then you'll need to talk to your mother about the specifics."

That part made my stomach turn. My mother was going to be so hurt that I was even entertaining this. And it wasn't likely that I would be able to get a straight answer out of her anyway. "But when I brought it up at lunch, she had a meltdown."

"Of course she did." Cynthia glanced toward the back of the salon where Wanda was putting the finishing touches on my mother's hair. "I know your mother is really sick, but what better time to ramp up your illness than when there's something heavy you don't want to deal with? That's what I meant when I said Mama Connie was running game. Trust your gut. You know when she's lucid and when she's not," Cynthia said. "So if I were you, I would do my best, in one of those moments when she has all of her faculties working properly, and call her out on it."

"That's what I did at lunch," I said.

"No, that's what you tried to do. And she turned on the water-works and you caved. Stand strong and demand answers."

Even as she spoke those words, I knew that was something I wouldn't be able to do. Not only had I been raised to revere my elders, I knew how much my mother loved me, and anything that brought her pain was hard for me. Cynthia must have known it too because she said, "Okay, if you can't do that, you have at least got to go talk to these people."

"And say what?" I asked.

"Well, obviously they think you're their daughter so go talk to them and tell them to prove it."

"I'm just trying to figure out why they would make something like this up?"

"They wouldn't," she said. "And with everything else you told me not adding up, I don't think the question is, 'are you or aren't you their daughter?' It's what are you going to do about the fact that you are?"

That made my insides turn somersaults. I paused as my mother walked back over to us. Cynthia flashed a wide smile.

"Well look at you, Mama Connie. Don't you just look like a doll?"

My mother fluffed her curls. "Yes, Wanda did a great job."

I forced a smile as well. "And she didn't even take long," I said. It had been difficult to get my mother to change her beautician but coming to Wanda was a lot easier on me because it was right down the street from our town house.

"Your dad is going to love this hair style," my mom said, leaning in and surveying herself in the mirror.

Cynthia and I exchanged glances. Mama had been doing fine when we arrived at the beauty shop a couple of hours ago. So now I was wondering if there was some legitimacy to what Cynthia was saying about my mother playing me.

Finally I said, "Mama, you know Daddy is dead?"

She paused and frowned and the pain on her face let me know that this episode was real. "He is?"

"Yes, for a very long time," I said, nodding.

The tears welled up in my mother's eyes. This is what I hated about the disease that was invading her mind. She relived the saddest moments of her life, over and over.

"Oh my," she said. "I-I have to go to the bathroom." She dabbed at her eyes and scurried away.

Cynthia shook her head as sympathy filled her face. "Dang, girl. I feel bad for you. You're right, though. It's going to kill her for you to go through with this."

"Hey, Cynthia. I'm ready for you," Wanda said, waving my best friend over.

Cynthia stood, looked at me, and took my hand, "But you have to do it." She squeezed. "Even if you don't tell your mother that you are doing it. You have to get some answers for yourself or you'll wonder for the rest of your life and no one wants a life of what ifs."

I knew my friend was right. But I also knew those answers wouldn't come from my mother. I opened my purse up, reached inside and pulled out Major Logan's card.

It was time to call him and get the answers I desperately needed.

Chapter 13

I couldn't believe I was here. Standing on the porch of Olympia Estates, one of the richest neighborhoods in Beaumont, Texas. I hadn't even told Malcolm that I was coming here. I'd driven the hour and a half this morning after arranging a meeting with Major and Elaine Logan. I was surprised to learn that they lived in Beaumont, a small town about 120 miles outside of Houston. I thought of Major's three-times-a-week visits to Starbucks over the past two months. Who would be that committed? As soon as the thought entered my mind, I knew—a father in search of answers.

Looking around the massive estate, it dawned on me that if this story was true, this should have been my home. I didn't know whether to cry or be angry. This place looked like it belonged in the centerfold of *Better Homes & Gardens*. The house had to have at least seven bedrooms. The Mediterranean-style home was the largest on the street in this gated community and sat on at least three acres. Spotlights illuminated the concrete walkway that bore stones which looked like they'd been imported from some country I couldn't pronounce.

I shook off my awe and rang the doorbell. I couldn't get caught up in the material trappings because if this story were true . . . I let my thoughts trail off as the door opened. Major stood there with a giant grin on his face.

"Hello, Jillian," he said. I instantly noticed that he'd said my whole first name. I was only Jill at work. As far as any customers knew, that was my name. But then again, a man like Major Logan would have thoroughly done his homework, so of course he would know my whole name.

"Um . . . hi," I said.

Major took a deep breath and before I could reply, he pulled me into his grasp. I didn't know whether to hug him back, so I did what felt natural and kept my arms at my sides.

"Come on in," he said, leading me into a massive foyer. I followed him down a long, narrow hallway into what looked like the living room. There was a wrought-iron, winding staircase with entrances from both sides. To my right were elegant wrought-iron double doors, leading to what I assumed was an office. I looked around at the dramatic high ceilings, countless crystal chandeliers, marble and wood flooring, and suddenly I felt so out of place.

"Hold on, have a seat right there." He pointed to a wingback chair that looked like it cost more than my car. "Let me go get your . . ." Major paused, "my wife. As you can imagine, she's very nervous about this meeting."

"I am, too," I mumbled, as he turned and hurried out of the room. The inside of this home was just as beautiful as the outside, if not more, from the obviously imported chandeliers to the designer furniture, the likes of which I'd only seen in magazines. Everything in this home screamed money. Lots of it.

I had just taken a seat when Major returned. He stepped to the side, revealing his wife. She looked like once upon a time, she could have been a supermodel. But the hollow look in her eyes told of years of heartache. Today, though, she looked different from that day in the car. Today, she looked . . . relieved.

"Hello," I said, if for no other reason than to break the awkward silence.

"So good to see you again," she said with a smile.

I couldn't be sure, because Major was holding her up, but it looked like Elaine was trembling. She took measured steps toward me. Her hand went immediately to my face and I didn't know how to react. She ran her fingers over my cheeks, used her other hand to brush my hair. Her eyes filled with tears and then she said, "My God. My baby," as she pulled me toward her.

Again, I didn't know whether to hug her or stand there. But because of the intensity of her hug, my hand slowly rose to the small of her back. And while she hugged, I patted. But she didn't seem to notice.

She stepped back, looked at my face, and then hugged me again. "I never gave up hope," she said.

"Okay, sweetheart. Let her breathe." I felt Major pulling her away and she gripped me tightly, almost as if she was scared if she released me, she would lose me again. Part of me felt a pain inside because this woman had been holding out hope and when I turned out not to be her daughter, this was going to be heartbreaking for her. Because even though I was here; even though my birth certificate and social security numbers appeared to be fake; and even though their story seemed legitimate—I had convinced myself that my mother was not a kidnapper. I was only here now to verify that fact.

"Please, have a seat," Major said. He was giddy with excitement. "Would you like something to drink?"

I shook my head. I seemed to have lost my voice since that hello.

"I know this is awkward," Major began as he and his wife sat down on the sofa across from me. "And we have so much to talk about."

Mrs. Logan looked at me and said bluntly, "Were you taken care of?"

"Excuse me?" I said, finally finding my words.

"Your life? Did you have a good life?" she asked.

I nodded. "I did."

That brought a smile, and a mist to her eyes. "Good."

"Look, we know you have questions for us. We have questions for you, too," Major said, taking his wife's hand.

I needed to nip this family reunion in the bud so my voice was firm as I said, "Well, I have to start with the fact that I'm not convinced I'm your daughter."

Those words seemed to be a dagger to Mrs. Logan's heart, because she clutched Major's arm. But then, she said with conviction, "You are." She pointed toward the fireplace, at an empty gold frame which sat on top of the mantle.

"That photo frame has sat there empty for the past twenty-six years, because you were stolen from me. From us. I carried you in my womb, so whether you realize it or not, we have a connection. I felt it the moment that I laid eyes on you in the back seat of our car. But I know you can feel it, too."

Major squeezed her hand and she instantly slowed her rising pace.

I wanted to tell this poor woman that I didn't understand anything except the fact that desperation was making her delusional. "I understand that you think I am your daughter," I said, "but again, my mother is Connie Harrison." The mention of my mother's name wiped the smile right off Mrs. Logan's face.

"That woman is a kid—" Major squeezed Mrs. Logan's hand again and she stopped talking mid-sentence.

He jumped in. "We understand that and we know nothing is for sure until you have a DNA test. But trust me, when I first discovered you, I did my research. There is no record of a Connie Harrison giving birth. In fact, there is no record of a Connie Harrison *or* a Jillian Harrison."

Now I knew they were crazy. They were trying to say not only was I not who I thought I was, but neither was my mother? Give me a break.

"Trust us," Mrs. Logan interjected, "we wouldn't have approached you if we weren't already sure. But as we said earlier, we do have a doctor here ready to conduct a DNA test."

On cue, an older gentleman with copper-colored hair and a lab coat emerged from the hallway.

"This is Dr. Maximillian Winters." Major handed me a Manila file, which I took. "He is the director of DNA Labquest, one of the most esteemed DNA facilities in the country. His credentials are there in the folder."

I glanced at all the paperwork, which looked like the dossier for a high-level NASA position.

"You want me to take a test now?" I said, taking in the three sets of eyes peering at me. "And you expect me to just trust someone you chose?"

There was indignation in Dr. Winters's voice as he said, "I assure you, I am completely professional and stand by the accuracy of my tests, though you are more than welcome to have subsequent tests at any facility of your choice."

Major stepped closer to me. "And yes, we'd like to take the test now. I'm sure you can understand that we all want answers as soon as possible."

"I already know the answer," Mrs. Logan said, her tone confident.

I closed the folder. "How do I know this test will be accurate?" I asked. When Major had first mentioned a DNA test over the phone, I'd balked. But the entire drive here, I kept telling myself that a test was the only way I'd get answers. I just didn't expect to be taking that test today.

"My aunt and uncle aren't in the business of picking random people off the street and faking DNA tests."

I turned to the voice of the young man walking into the living room. He, too, emerged as if he had been awaiting the right moment. The man looked like he was in his early twenties and wasn't any taller than five-four. He wore a tweed blazer and round glasses and a scowl that made evident his feelings about my presence.

"Phillip, don't be rude," Major said, his voice chastising.

"I'm sorry, Uncle. I'm not completely onboard with these shenanigans," he said, shaking his head as he walked over to me, stood in front of me, then did a whole body scan with one glare.

I frowned at him as I debated how much of my time he was worth.

"This is my nephew, Phillip," Major said. "My sister's son. He has been with us since he was six. We raised him as our own after my sister's death."

Phillip had the audacity to walk around me, his eyes roaming up and down like he was studying some slave on an auction block. "And I'm very protective of my aunt and uncle," he said. "And very much aware of people that try to take advantage of their wealth."

Major waved off his nephew's words. "We are blessed financially," he said. "I have made some good investments and Elaine's family has done well in the manufacturing industry. We're well off but we are not extremely wealthy people."

I glanced around the massive home. If this wasn't wealthy, I didn't know what was.

"Regardless, we are also cognizant of the games people play." Phillip stopped his examination and folded his arms across his chest.

"Look, what's your name again?" I asked.

"Phillip Logan," he said with authority, like he was used to spouting his name and instantly commanding respect.

"Phillip," I repeated, not bothering to hide my disdain. "I didn't come after your aunt and uncle. They came after me."

"That's how scam artists usually set things up."

"Are you serious?" I asked.

"Okay, everybody calm down," Major said. "This is a joyous occasion."

"Well, I just think those individuals that you invite into our home, your life, should be more fully vetted," Phillip said, his voice dripping with disdain.

"You know what?" I snapped, "A week ago, I didn't even know you people. But you know what, let's go ahead and have your doctor administer this DNA test so that I can put an end to this." I turned to Mrs. Logan. "And I am so sorry that you're having to endure this, but hopefully it will give you some closure as you search for your real daughter."

Those words looked like they pained her but she simply nodded. I turned to Dr. Winters. "Let's get this over with, please."

They had no idea. I was suddenly anxious to put an end to this outlandish theory, chalk all of these unanswered questions up to coincidences, and then go back and resume my life.

Chapter 14

The piece of paper trembled in my hand. I had to have memorized every number, every letter, every percentage point on this paper. I'd analyzed and scrutinized all the ways that this could be wrong but in my heart I knew it was right.

Major had shown up at my job this morning, papers in hand, ready to take a family portrait. It had been forty-eight hours since we'd taken the test and I knew he was anxious. He'd wanted me to open the sealed envelope right there in Starbucks, but I'd refused. My gut already knew what the paper said and I didn't need my co-workers seeing me have a meltdown.

But if I was to have a meltdown, Major and Elaine would be right there to see it all, because they sat out in the parking lot until I finished my shift.

I was full of trepidation as I headed out to their car after I finally got off. There was no driver this time. Just Major and Elaine, and just like last time, she was in the back seat. Judging by the antsy looks on their faces, I could tell they had no idea what the paper said.

"Are you ready?" Major asked me after I was seated in the back seat next to his wife. We'd all agreed that we would open the results together.

"I guess," I said, my voice soft. He handed the envelope to me.

I turned it over and studied it to make sure the seal hadn't been tampered with. When I was sure that it hadn't, I flipped the envelope back over and opened it. When I'd pulled the results out of the envelope, silence filled the car as everyone waited with bated breath.

My eyes scanned the numbers that meant nothing to me . . . I went to the bottom of the page to a paragraph that said "Conclusion." My heart dropped at the third paragraph:

Assuming the specimens are from the persons indicated, the alleged father, Major Logan, cannot be excluded as the biological father of the child, Jillian Harrison, since they share genetic markers. Using the above systems, the probability of paternity is 99.9999%. . . .

"Oh my. God," I whispered.

Elaine gently took the paper from my hand.

"Thank you, God!" she shouted, reaching over and hugging me as a cascade of tears tumbled down her cheeks. "I knew it. I just knew it!"

"Our daughter is home!" Major said, reaching over the seat to squeeze my hand.

I was numb for the next twenty minutes. Major and Elaine were making plans—talking about Elaine and me meeting up for lunch for some one-on-one, mother-daughter bonding time, their meeting Destiny and being grandparents—and all I could think was one thing: My whole life was a lie.

⟶⋗•⋖⟵

I'd left the Logans, crying all the way home. And now, I had been sitting in front of my town house for the last hour. I was unable to go inside because I didn't know how I could look the woman who I thought was my mother in the eyes.

Maybe I was switched at birth, I told myself. *Maybe my mother didn't know I wasn't her biological child. Maybe anything,* I thought. Because there was no way my mother could be a kidnapper.

I'd been contemplating all kinds of maybes on my drive home. But none of them were giving me solace.

I made my way inside the town house just in time for Malcolm to say, "Okay, I'm glad you got back here. I was wondering if I would make it in time for this second interview."

I'd been so caught up in my drama that I'd forgotten that he had a callback interview. "Sorry, baby," I said, giving him a quick peck on the cheek.

"Are you okay?" he asked, studying me. My husband could be in his own world, especially when he was working on his app. But he had this uncanny knack to be directly in tune with me.

I nodded. I knew I needed to share these results with him, but right now, I was just numb. Right now, I didn't know what to say. Besides, I needed him to focus on his interview.

"Where's Mama?" I asked.

"She's in her room playing with Destiny."

"Alone?" I asked.

He nodded as he adjusted his tie. "Yeah, she's been doing pretty good all day."

Normally, that declaration would have had me feeling good but today, I had mixed emotions about that. Maybe if my mother was in her right mind, I could get some answers. And then again, maybe my questions would send her over the edge. Either way, I knew that I had to find a way to approach my mother with this, no matter what the outcome.

"Don't forget dinner at my mom's tonight," Malcom reminded me. "I told her we'd be there by seven. I already called Aunt Marilyn. She'll be over here to watch your mother by six."

I kissed Malcolm goodbye, took a deep breath, and then headed toward my mother's bedroom.

"Hey, Mama," I said, easing her door open. The paper was now folded in a trifold in my hand.

"Hello, sweetheart," my mother said. She glanced over at my daughter, fast asleep on her bed. "You see Destiny has dozed off and gone to sleep. I'm just sitting here reading." I smiled at the book in her hand.

"I'm glad you got back into reading," I said. Growing up, my mother had ignited my love of books by reading to me every chance she had. We couldn't afford to travel, but we would explore the world through the pages of a book. That was yet another thing dementia had robbed her of—her love of reading.

"Yeah. Oprah recommended this book called *American Marriage*. It's good but it's hard when you can't always follow along . . ." She let her words trail off.

"Mama, I need to speak to you about something."

She set her book down and tucked the little blanket around Destiny, and then eased off the bed.

"Okay. Destiny is sound asleep. Let's talk out here so we don't wake her."

I followed my mother out into the hallway. "Let's go into my room," I said.

"Is everything okay?" she asked me after we were in my room. "Are you and Malcolm having problems?"

"No, no," I said, shifting my weight from one foot to the other. "Nothing like that." I swallowed, then released a breath. "Mama, tell me about my daddy again."

She narrowed her eyed in confusion. "What? Why do you want me to rehash that story?"

"I don't know." I shrugged. "Just trying to figure some things out."

"Well, your dad loved you very much," she said with a nostalgic smile. "And I do, too. I don't know why we're having this conversation."

I unfolded the paper and extended it toward her. "My birth

has never really added up. But, you always had an excuse for the inconsistencies," I told her. "But this . . ."

"What is this?" she asked, taking the paper.

"It's a paternity test."

"What?" she exclaimed, her eyes widened in shock as she eased down onto the bed.

"The man who showed up at my job last week and said he's my father," I continued before I lost my nerve.

"And you believed him? And you took a paternity test?" She looked up at me in shock.

I studied her, trying to gauge her reaction, search for some hint of . . . something that could explain this.

I moved closer so that I was standing right over her. "Mama, I need you to look me in my eyes and tell me the truth."

My mother looked up and with a wide smile said with conviction, "Jilly, I promise you. You are my daughter."

That made me smile as well. Test or no test, Connie Harrison was my mother. I just needed to make sense of this birth revelation and figure out how this mix-up happened.

Chapter 15

If Kendra was upset about the fiasco at her wedding, she wasn't showing it. I'd been apprehensive about joining Malcolm and his family for their monthly family dinner. Normally, we held them on Sundays, but this week Mrs. Reed was doing it on Friday because it was Kendra's birthday.

This was going to be the first time we'd all been together since Mama had ruined (or almost ruined) Kendra's wedding. I was prepared for the cold shoulder from everyone—including my dear friend of fifteen years. But the way Kendra embraced me when we arrived let me know that she wasn't harboring any ill will.

"Girl, why haven't you been in touch?" she asked. "I haven't had a chance to tell you about the fabulous honeymoon or anything."

"I—I don't know. I was just trying to give you some space." I sighed. "Look, Kendra. I'm really sorry—"

She cut me off and said, "We're here to have a good time and celebrate my birthday. You know I don't live in the past. And you know I have nothing but love for Mama Connie."

That brought a smile to my face. "Come on and let me show you these pictures from our honeymoon," she continued. And just like that, we slipped back into old times.

We'd been there about an hour when Mrs. Reed summoned us for dinner. I marveled as I watched the ease with which Malcolm and his siblings all fell into their respective places. Kendra and Travis, me and Malcolm, his brother Clay and Clay's girlfriend of the week, and their brother Billy. I always loved being around them because they were the definition of a family. They laughed together, played together, and if you dared cross one of them you'd have to deal with them all.

Billy started talking about his date last night and had everybody at the table cracking up. "And I kid you not, she has three teeth," he said.

"Billy, stop lying." Mrs. Reed said.

"Mama you know he's always making up stuff. The boy should have been a fiction writer," Malcolm said.

"I should have been because my life is a best seller." Billy laughed.

I smiled as I watched the banter between them. Being here made me sad from time to time because it made me wish that I'd had a sibling to fight with, a sister to steal clothes from, a brother to aggravate. Granted, I enjoyed my time with Mama, but it made me question the definition of a family. Could you really have a family with just two people? That's what it had been with me and Mama. I don't know why, but I started thinking about the Logans. What if I had not been kidnapped, would they have had more kids? Would I have gone to private school, an Ivy League college, married someone other than Malcolm? That latter part made me feel like my life had unfolded just as it was meant to because I couldn't imagine being married to anyone other than Malcolm. But I couldn't help but wonder about the what-ifs.

After we wrapped up dinner and said our goodbyes, Malcolm took my hand as we walked to the car. Once we were inside and heading down Highway 6, he asked, "Babe, what's going on? You didn't seem like yourself the entire time."

I gave him a smile. "I'm so sorry." I took a deep breath as we passed a luxury car just like the one Mr. Logan had. "I need to talk to you about something."

My tone must've worried him because he studied me for a moment, then said, "Hold on," and pulled over in a Target parking lot. "What's going on, babe?"

"I have been out of it because . . ." I inhaled again.

"Yes?" he motioned for me to continue. I took my husband's hand and squeezed it. "Babe, you're scaring me. What's going on?" he said.

"I met with the Logans," I said with a sigh.

"What?" he said. "Why didn't you tell me?"

I shrugged. "I don't know. It all happened so fast. I didn't want to tell you before your interview. Then when you got back we were running late for dinner. Anyway, I went down there to tell them that they made a big mistake."

"Down where?"

"They live in Beaumont. I went to just talk to them and tell them they made a mistake and then their nephew, Phillip, just started making all these snide remarks." I stopped talking for a moment, took a deep breath, and then continued. "Next thing I know, I was taking a DNA test." I rushed the words out.

"What?" he exclaimed. "All of this was going on and you didn't tell me?"

I hoped he didn't get angry because right then, I couldn't deal with that on top of everything else. "I'm telling you now. It's just been overwhelming," I replied.

"Okay." I could tell he was trying to control his emotions. "So, what did the DNA test say?"

I turned to face him, fought back my tears, and said, "I'm not who I thought I was. The DNA was a match with Major Logan."

That caused Malcolm to fall back onto the seat. "I knew it. I knew it," he said, then took my hands. "Babe, I'm sorry you have to go through this." He kissed my fingers.

"It's just so many questions. I have so many questions," I said.

"Well, now we know," Malcolm replied. "So the key thing is for us to get some answers, and I'm with you every step of the way."

Usually, that made me feel better. Not this time. This time, I couldn't help but feel we both were in for a rocky journey.

Chapter 16

Maybe I should have left my husband at home. Yes, I wanted Malcolm by my side as I was officially introduced to the Logan family. I knew he would immediately be enamored, and that could potentially cloud his judgment. And judging from his wide eyes as we pulled up in front of the Logans' massive home, I had been right.

"Wow," he said as we pulled into the Logans' gate, drove up the mile-long driveway and onto the sprawling estate.

"I told you it was nice," I said as I motioned for him to park in the circular driveway, then led him up the walkway.

"So you mean to tell me this is how you should have really been living?" he whispered after we were out of the car and walking up the stairs that led to the mahogany double front door.

I took a deep breath and struggled to fight off my irritation at my husband. It was only natural that he would be in awe of this place. But this was a life-changing experience for me. I needed his head clear and I didn't want to be sidetracked by the material things. The Logans had insisted that I bring Malcolm to dinner so that they could meet him. They wanted me to bring Destiny, too. Even though she really wouldn't understand what was going on, I wasn't ready for that, so the sitter was at my house watching both my mother and daughter.

"I lived how I should have been living," I replied. The one thing I didn't want was to have the Logan money make me lose sight of the life I had built with my mother. No, it had not been rich in material things, but it had been rich in love and I didn't want that overshadowed by the wealth of the Logans.

"Did you ring the doorbell?" Malcolm asked. He was shifting like he was antsy.

"I did and will you calm down?" I told him.

He rubbed his palms on his jeans. "I'm trying. I just can't believe this . . . And . . ." He motioned around the palatial estate. "This. It's all just so overwhelming."

"I know," I said, biting my bottom lip as I turned my attention back to the door.

Malcolm must've noticed my expression and remembered this day was about me, because he took me in his arms. "I got you, babe. I know you're conflicted about this, but you said yourself that you want to know who you are. And it's time for you to do that."

I nodded as he leaned in and kissed my forehead just as the door opened.

"Hello," said a woman wearing a maid's uniform. I didn't even realize black people had maids like on TV. "Mr. and Mrs. Logan are expecting you." She spun and motioned for us to follow her. We walked down the long hallway. This time, we turned left into the dining room versus right to the study that I was in the last time I was here.

I heard the chatter of several people coming from the dining room. As we rounded a corner, Major appeared.

"Jill, so nice to see you," he said, embracing me. "And you must be Malcolm?" He extended his hand and fiercely shook Malcolm's hand.

Malcolm returned his enthusiastic greeting. "Yes, sir. It's nice to meet you."

"It is my pleasure," he replied. "I'm so looking forward to learning more about," he paused as if he was trying to make sure it was okay to say the next words, "my son-in-law."

Malcolm shifted uneasily, like he didn't know how to process that. He looked over at me to gauge my reaction. I had none.

"Well, come on in," Major said, motioning toward the dining area. "Several people are here. All of them are excited about Alicia, I mean, Jill's return."

I cringed. For twenty-seven years, I'd been Jillian. Surely these people didn't expect me to suddenly accept being "Alicia."

As we walked behind Major into the dining room, I couldn't help but wonder if maybe we should have done this alone. Not around all of these people, whoever they were. This was not only a private moment, it was a difficult one. I didn't need a room full of strangers studying and dissecting me.

But it was too late now. There had to be two dozen people in the room. A mixture of people: old and young, black and white. There was a man who looked like a college professor and several prim and proper women sitting around the large oak table, which was adorned with enough food to feed the entire Buffalo Soldiers army.

Major immediately began introducing me to people around the room.

"This is my brother, your uncle Dave," he said, pointing to the professor. "This is Martha and Emerson, they are your godparents," he continued, pointing to a couple sitting on the right side of the table.

For the next ten minutes it went like that, Major introducing people who were supposed to matter to me. I don't think I remembered anybody's name, and I hated how they were all studying me like I was some kind of special assignment. We'd just finished the last of the introductions when Elaine entered the room.

"You're here!" she exclaimed, hugging me. "That is so wonderful. It is so great to see you. I've been anxiously waiting all day." Then she walked over and hugged Malcolm. "And it's a pleasure to meet you." She turned back to me. "I trust you've had a chance to meet your family." She didn't give me time to reply before she said, "Come. Come," as she took my arm. "I saved you a seat right next to me."

I glanced back at Malcolm as she dragged me to the table. For the next hour while we dined on Peking duck and other dishes I had never heard of, I felt like I was in a whirlwind situation. I was bombarded with questions, showered with praise and doted on like a china doll. It all made me uneasy.

Malcolm, however, looked like he had been a part of their family his whole life. He laughed with them, cracked jokes, and fit right in.

Yeah, I definitely should have left him at home. No way would he be objective in this situation. And it's not like I even knew how I wanted him to react. I just wanted him to do it with a clear mind.

Not that I didn't want Malcolm to get to know my family; I paused as I realized that I had just thought of them as my family. I shook my head trying to come to terms with that new reality.

"So, Alicia," the professor-looking man asked, "where did you go to college?"

"Dave, she goes by Jill," Major said.

"Because Jill is my name," I couldn't help but add.

"Pardon me," Dave corrected. "Jill. Where did you attend college?"

Major smiled at me. "Your uncle teaches eighteenth century World History and British Literature at Rice University."

"I attended TSU for a while, but I didn't finish," I replied.

He looked unimpressed and Elaine stepped in.

"Our . . . Jill has had an eventful life that I'm sure one day she'll be happy to share with us all," Elaine said. "For now, let's just enjoy this fine meal."

That seemed to settle everyone and the conversation changed to more generic topics. Malcolm was telling some of the family members about his app when I looked down at my vibrating phone. My heart dropped when I saw, "Fort Bend County Sheriff" on the Caller ID.

"Please excuse me," I said, scooting back from the table.

"Where are you going, dear?" Elaine asked.

"I have to answer this phone call."

"We generally don't bring our cell phones to the dinner table," she said, a firm smile across her face.

"It is quite rude," Dave mumbled with disgust.

"Give her a pass," someone else at the table said. "It's not like she grew up with any proper training."

The way several people giggled in response made me angry, but I didn't have time to deal with them, or my husband, who while he didn't laugh, didn't come to my defense either. I ignored all of them as I pressed the Talk button and stepped into the hall.

"Hello," I said.

"Is this Jill Reed?" the voice on the other end asked.

"Yes, may I help you?"

"Mrs. Reed, we got your number from our database. We have a woman here who we believe is your mother."

"Oh my God," I said. "Where is here?"

"At the Sheriff's office in Richmond."

"Richmond?" I asked. That was at least thirty-five minutes from us.

"Is she all right?"

"We believe so. She is very disoriented. But we're grateful that's all she is."

"What does that mean?"

"Would it be possible for you to come to the police station?"

I didn't hesitate as I said, "I'm on my way."

I was sure Elaine would be upset, but this mini family reunion would have to wait. My mother needed me. And I didn't see how anything would ever change that fact.

Chapter 17

My heart raced as I jumped out of the car and bolted up the stairs to the Fort Bend Sheriff's Department. The place was a bevy of activity, with drunks, hookers, and defiant-looking juvenile delinquents scattered about.

I looked to my right, then my left; when I noticed the reception desk, I darted over.

"Hello, my name is Jill Reed," I said, trying to catch my breath. "I got a call that my mother, Connie Harrison, is here at the police station. Apparently, she was picked up by the cops."

The officer at the front desk tapped the computer screen. "Yes, it looks like she's in holding," he said. "Please have a seat."

"Holding? Why is she in holding? What happened?" The man was so casual as he spoke, but I was a frantic mess.

The officer pointed to a row of chairs on the other side of the room. "Ma'am, please have a seat and someone will be with you shortly."

I felt Malcolm's hand go to the small of my back. I'd left him in the parking lot and hadn't even realized that he had caught up with me. "Babe, calm down. I'm sure she's fine. We'll get answers in a minute."

My hands trembled in nervousness. My mother was probably

dazed and confused and freaking out and all I could think was what in the world had she done to get arrested.

It seemed like an eternity before someone finally came out.

"Jill Reed?" the officer said.

"Yes, that's me," I said, jumping up.

"Come with me, please."

The officer turned and led us down a long hallway. When we reached the end, he took us into a small conference room. "It seems your neighbors at 3007 South Gessner say your mother attempted to break in to their apartment. When they opened the door, she became agitated, saying they were in her apartment and that they'd killed her family. She has an identity bracelet on, which is registered to our district here in Richmond."

I let out a heavy sigh. Aunt Marilyn had given my mother the bracelet so she must've had it registered to her address in Richmond. "My mother suffers from dementia," I said. "She gets very confused. It's the same apartment as ours. It's just a different building."

"I figured as much, but your mother was in a highly emotional state. To the point that we were concerned about her safety." He looked down at his clipboard. "About thirty minutes ago, she was transported to Ben Taub Hospital."

"She's in the hospital? Why couldn't they tell us that before we came here?"

The officer ignored my question and handed us a Post-it. "Here's the information for the hospital. It doesn't appear that your mother should be left alone. She really could've done some damage, or worse, gotten hurt. Your mother was so belligerent that the homeowners would've been well within their rights to protect their property."

The thought of some panicked resident blasting a shotgun into my mother terrified me. Malcolm pulled me to him and hugged me. "Come on, babe. Let's go to the hospital."

"Thank you, officer. Is my mother going to face any charges?"

"No, I'll do the paperwork to clear all of this up." The officer flashed a chastising look. "But, Mrs. Reed, I suggest you do something, or this story could be ending very differently."

I nodded without replying.

Thirty minutes later we were at Ben Taub Hospital. After having been directed to my mother's room, I found her fast asleep. Tears sprang to my eyes as I walked over and stroked her hair. The movement caused her to stir. Her eyes fluttered and she slowly looked up at me. A small smile formed.

"Jill?" she whispered.

"Yes, Mama, I'm here."

"You're always here. Thank God, you're always here." She shifted to get comfortable as she squeezed my hand tighter. "I think I got turned around. We don't live in a nice neighborhood, Jill. That man was so mean. He cursed me and pushed me down."

"But you're okay now."

She closed her eyes and I saw the slow rise and fall of her chest. "I'm always okay as long as I have you. I love you, Jill."

I leaned in and kissed her on her forehead. "I love you, too, Mama."

———

My husband shifted my daughter from one side of his chest to the other. She mumbled gibberish and briefly opened her eyes before closing them right back.

I took the keys out of his hand and opened the door. I knew he was irritated with having to leave the dinner and spend our evening at the hospital, but I didn't know what else he expected me to do. Luckily, Mom was going to be fine and Malcolm took me home to get my car and a change of clothes so I could go back up to the hospital.

I unlocked the door, then made my way inside as he followed. I flipped the switch to turn the lights on.

"Let me warm Destiny's bottle because I know she's starving," I said, heading over to the kitchen sink. I turned the faucet on and nothing happened. A sinking feeling immediately engulfed me.

"What's up?" Malcolm said. "Are you going to warm her bottle?"

"I tried," I said, turning to face him. "It looks like the water has been cut off."

He released a string of curse words as he laid Destiny down on the sofa, then as if he needed to verify himself, he went over to the sink and tried to turn the faucet on.

"Damn it," he said. "I thought we'd at least have until the end of the week."

"I thought you said you made payment arrangements," I said.

"I did," he snapped. "I asked them to give me until Friday. They said because it was a rollover bill they couldn't make any promises. It seems like they should give us some kind of warning," he said, kicking the ottoman like it was the furniture's fault.

I wanted to remind him that the warning had been the pink disconnection notice lying on the counter. Instead, I just said, "It's okay, baby. I'll just warm it in the microwave. This one time won't kill her."

"It's not okay," he yelled. "We're in this place, struggling, and I'm sick of it," he continued. "What kind of man am I when I can't even keep the water on in my own damn house?"

"Malcolm, calm down, baby," I said, reaching out to him. He jerked his arm away and I knew that his anger wasn't directed at me. My husband had been trying hard, but he just couldn't catch a break. "It's okay, we're going to be fine," I told him.

He sat down at the kitchen table as I put Destiny's bottle in the microwave. I had never seen my husband look so dejected. I waited for the beep, checked the heat of the bottle, then made my way back over to the sofa to pick Destiny up and take her to her swing.

"The water bill was ninety-three dollars. Ninety-three freaking dollars and we don't have it. And we don't even have anybody we can go borrow it from," he said.

We had wiped out my mom's social security check paying the other past due bills. It was not like she had much anyway. And Malcolm would die rather than ask his mother or siblings.

"We'll figure something out," I said.

"We just left a mansion and we come home to our water being shut off." Malcolm released a pained laugh.

I weighed my words carefully as I said what I was totally against but didn't know if it was what he wanted to hear. "Uh, Malcolm, I can't ask them for any money."

"Why not? They're your family," he protested, his voice filled with exasperation.

"Family that I just met," I reminded him. My tone was low, like I was trying to reason with him. "You don't want to ask your family and you've known them all your life. I can't ask these people that I barely know."

He inhaled, then let out a long slow breath. "I know that, babe. I know you would never feel comfortable, but . . ." He took a deep breath. "I understand. This is all just so frustrating."

"We'll figure something out, baby. We always do." I sat on the sofa next to him and buried my head in the crevice of his arms as he held me tightly until we both dozed off from exhaustion.

I don't know how long Malcolm and I had been asleep, but the sound of screaming caused us to jump up.

"What is that?" Malcolm asked.

Before I could reply, we heard a splatter of gunshots and both of us dove onto the floor. Malcolm scurried over to Destiny, snatched her out of her swing and used his body to completely shield her. The window in our front room shattered. My screams mixed with Destiny's wailing.

We heard someone from outside yell, "Let's go, he got the message!"

I don't know how long we lay on the floor, but my heart raced in panic. Even Destiny had stopped hollering and was trembling in fear. After a few minutes, Malcolm scooted Destiny toward me. "Take her upstairs," he whispered.

"Where are you going?"

He eased toward the window and looked outside. "The cops are here. It's okay. They're at the neighbor's two doors down." His shoulders slumped in relief.

I breathed a sigh of relief as I stood up. Destiny just stared at me wide-eyed, terror on her tiny face.

As I looked down at my baby girl, I knew my mother was right; this place was no longer safe and we needed to get the hell of out of here. I hugged my daughter tight and scurried up the stairs.

Chapter 18

My best friend paced back and forth across my living room floor like I was a lost cause.

"So, I just paid the water bill," she said. "They said it should be back on in the next hour. I cannot have my bestie walking around with funky breath because she doesn't even have water to brush her teeth. I can't believe you didn't borrow the money from me."

"Because I already owe you a hundred dollars," I replied, rubbing my temples, exasperated over the previous day's events. Malcolm had given a statement to the police about what he heard but thank goodness, he didn't actually see anything because the last thing we needed was someone trying to come and retaliate against us.

Cynthia waved me off as she continued. "I don't care about that. I can't believe someone shot your place up. My God," she looked around frantically, "is it even safe to be here?" She peered at the wall over the sofa. "Holy cow, are those bullet holes?"

I nodded. Malcolm had discovered those this morning, three perfectly round holes. The police were supposed to be coming back later to retrieve the bullets.

"Yeah, Malcolm and I agreed we have to do something. Both the guy next door and the guy down the hall are into some illicit stuff and I am worried sick that we're going to get caught in the crossfire," I replied.

"You need to be looking for another place, pronto," Cynthia said as she walked over to the window that we'd covered with a garbage bag the night before.

I said, "I know, but rent, deposit, moving expenses, it's just too much." Just the thought of all that made me want to cry.

Cynthia turned and looked at me. "Which brings me to my next point in this drama filled life of yours. You mean to tell me that your parents are stupid rich?"

I nodded.

She looked around my place. "And y'all living up in this . . ." I could tell that she was about to say something derogatory and caught herself. "This tiny place, dodging bullets," she said.

"This tiny place is our home," I said, defensively.

"Home is where you make it. And you need to be upstairs packing so you can make your way out of here and find somewhere else to live. Anywhere else."

"Where?" I huffed. "We can't afford to move. We can't afford anything." Malcolm had gotten up first thing this morning and after using a bottled water I'd brought from work last week to wash up and brush his teeth, he'd gone back to the garage he used to work at to try and get them to hire him. I know that was killing him, but as he told me before he'd left, "staying here was killing him more."

Cynthia waved my words away. "Girl, bye. I'm with Malcolm. You need to go claim what's rightfully yours. Do you know how different your life would be if you had grown up with what you're entitled to?"

Even though that thought had crossed my mind multiple times, I said, "I just feel funny about all of this. I don't know these people."

Cynthia plopped down on the sofa, then I guess she remembered the bullet holes and got up and moved to the chair on the other side of the room. "You don't know them yet," she said. "Get to know them. Obviously, they want you in their lives."

I sighed. "I know, but I just feel like I need to take it slow."

"Do you like living here?" she asked.

"Of course not," I replied.

"Do you like working at Starbucks?" she asked.

"You know I don't. I mean, ten years ago, I would've loved it. But I want a career."

"Then, go work for your daddy. Shoot, it worked for Ivanka Trump. What does he do again?"

"He works in manufacturing and apparently supplies goods to discount stores all over the country. He also has a bunch of other investments."

"Go work for his company. Start building a legacy for you and Destiny."

I knew my best friend was right, but something about this whole situation wasn't sitting right with me. My life could change, but I guess I felt like that would've been an admission of my mother's wrongdoing.

"Where's your mom?" Cynthia asked.

"Aunt Marilyn and one of her church friends are bringing her home from the hospital. I had to stay here for the people to come fix our window," I said.

"Oh, and Destiny?"

"She's with Malcolm's sister."

Cynthia turned up her nose. "And all of them left without baths?"

I rolled my eyes at my friend. "We used some bottled water to brush our teeth."

"You know that's crazy, right?" Cynthia retorted. "Especially considering your father is stupid rich."

I was just about to say something else to her when the doorbell rang.

"You're expecting somebody?" she asked.

"No." I shrugged. Outside of Malcolm's friends, no one ever

visited us. I walked over and glanced out the peephole. I turned to Cynthia, my eyes bugging. "It's Phillip," I whispered.

"Who is Phillip?" she asked.

"Major's nephew. My cousin, I guess."

"Well, open the door and let our rich family in. Is Phillip cute? Maybe I can get in this rich family, too." She wiggled her hips in anticipation, eliciting a chuckle for the first time in the past twenty-four hours.

I spun back toward the door. "Hello, Phillip," I said after I'd opened the door. "How are you?"

"I'm fine," he said, his nose turned up like the very sight of my small town home disgusted him. "I just happened to be in the neighborhood and wanted to drop by."

I narrowed my eyes at him. I didn't know what he was up to, but he was a horrible liar. "Oh, you just happened to be in my neighborhood?"

"Okay. So, I came over to see you," he confessed. "May I come in?"

I wanted to ask him if he was sure he wanted to do that since he was looking at my place with such disdain. But I was curious, so I stepped aside and motioned for him to come in.

"Well, hello," Cynthia said, sashaying over to him. She threw her burgundy braids over her shoulder and smiled in his direction. "I'm Cynthia, Jill's bestie."

"Do grown people say bestie?" he replied, his nose scrunched up.

Cynthia wasn't fazed by his rudeness. "I do. And you are?" she said, her seductive meter on ten.

Phillip didn't bother to shake her outstretched hand. He just looked at her, turned his nose up some more and said, "Not interested."

Cynthia dropped her hand, cocked her head and looked at me. "Did he really go there?" she asked.

"Chill for a minute, okay?" I replied. "I'm sure Phillip wasn't trying to be rude."

Phillip pursed his lips and didn't respond. "Look, I just stopped by because I would like to talk with you for a moment," he said, dismissing Cynthia.

"Talk to me about what?" I asked.

He looked over at Cynthia, like he expected her to leave the room. Instead Cynthia said, "Yeah, talk to us about what?"

"Not *us*," he said, not bothering to look at Cynthia. "Talk to *you*."

"Well, she's my best friend, so . . ."

"I would prefer to have this as a private conversation," he said, his irritation evident.

Cynthia stepped to the side of me. "Well, we don't really care what you prefer." Her desire to be a part of the Logan family was out the window and she'd brought out South Side Chicago Cynthia.

I looked at her and said, "Give us a minute. Okay?"

She rolled her eyes, looked Phillip up and down, and then hissed, "Ol' bougie, pint-sized . . ." she muttered as she walked off.

"Phillip, what can I help you with?" I asked once Cynthia had disappeared upstairs.

He sighed, brushed his tweed coat down, stood erect like he was about to recite a well-rehearsed speech and said, "Well, as you can imagine, your appearance has caught this family by surprise."

I folded my arms and glared at him. "Well, as you've been told countless times, I didn't seek them out. They sought me."

"I understand that." He rolled his eyes in exasperation. "My aunt has this desperate void that she's been trying to fill for years."

"Okay. And?"

"And my point is," he began pacing, "I am very protective of my aunt and uncle. And if I think for a moment you are trying to do something dirty—"

"Whoa, let me stop you," I said, holding up my hands to cut him off. "If I am indeed their child, we will deal with it then. But don't come walking into my house, hurling accusations at me."

"I just want to make sure we're on the same page." He paused, like he was thinking about how to say his next words. "I'm sure they will want to rewrite their will, so I simply want to make sure you're on the up and up."

I laughed. "Oh, that's what this is about? You're afraid that everything will no longer be left to you?"

He ignored my question as he looked around my place. His eyes widened at the sight of the shattered window and the holes in the wall. "Oh my God. Are those bullet holes?"

"What can I do for you, Phillip?" I really didn't have the stamina for this right now.

He pulled his coat closed, like he was scared someone was about to open fire again right then. "I didn't think this place looked safe. You can't possible by okay with raising your daughter in these conditions." He reached in his pocket and pulled out what looked like his checkbook. "How about I just write you a check for you to just forget this DNA nonsense with my aunt and uncle and tell them you have no interest in getting to know them. Then you and your family can go back to your normal . . ." he looked around my living room, ". . . drama-filled lives."

I couldn't believe the nerve of him. If I'd given one iota about the Logan money, I wouldn't be sitting here lamenting my bleak financial situation. "How about you get the hell out of my house?" I said.

"Jillian, I don't want things to be ugly between us," he replied. "I'm just trying . . ."

"Goodbye, Phillip. I have things to do." I walked over to the door and opened it, just as my aunt Marilyn and my mother walked up.

"Doggone it," I mumbled. I silently cursed. I really didn't want Phillip to see my mother. I tried to gauge her mental demeanor, but she was all smiles, so I couldn't really determine where her head was.

"Hi, Jill. Marilyn promised me teacakes today," my mother announced with a wide grin.

"Aunt Marilyn, I thought you were taking her to your place?"

"She insisted on coming home and I don't have the energy to fight with your mother."

"I wanted to come home," my mother said. She smiled when she saw Phillip standing behind me. "Oh hi, are you Jill's friend?"

Phillip didn't bother to smile as he said, "No, but I am an acquaintance. And you are?"

"I'm Jill's mother, Connie." Her voice was childlike as she said, "Did you go to school with my Jilly?"

"Your Jilly?" he said, a slow smile crossing his face. "I did not. I'm Ivy League educated. Cornell."

"Oh, I like their glass baking ware. They make the best cakes," she replied.

Phillip looked confused for a moment, then said, "I'm sorry, I don't understand."

"Cornell. I got the set last Christmas. Jill and Malcolm bought it for me. Do you bake?"

Phillip seemed like he was fighting back a chuckle. "Really?"

I took that opportunity to jump in. "Mom, why don't you go on inside. Aunt Marilyn, are you staying?"

Aunt Marilyn shook her head. "No. I'm exhausted. Sister Addie is taking me to dinner. This is all just too much for me. This dementia is going to be the death of us all." She sighed and headed back to her car.

"Bye, Aunt Marilyn!" my mother called out after her.

Aunt Marilyn waved over her shoulder, then disappeared around the corner.

"Jill, do you want some of my teacakes?" my mother asked.

"It's okay, Mama. Go on inside."

Phillip quickly stepped up. "You sound like you really love your daughter."

"Oh, I do. She's my heart." She walked over and kissed me on the cheek. "It's not many mothers that can say their daughter will never ever leave them. And Jilly will never ever leave me."

"Mom, go on upstairs. Cynthia is up there. She would love to see you. Maybe ask her if she feels like letting you braid her hair."

"Oh, that would be nice," my mother said. "Then maybe afterward, we can go see the new Sidney Poitier and Bill Cosby movie, *Let's Do it Again*. I heard it's really good." She smiled at Phillip. "Goodbye. What's your name again?"

"Phillip," he replied, still looking confused.

"Goodbye, Sam." My mother smiled and walked toward the stairs.

Phillip stood with a smirk on his face. "Your *mother* seems like a wonderful person. I would've never guessed that she was a cold-hearted kidnapper."

"Goodbye, Phillip," I said.

He smiled, turned and walked out the door. The twinkling in his eyes told me that meeting my mother had sent the wheels spinning in his head. And I didn't have a good feeling about what was to come.

Chapter 19

The maintenance man had fixed the window, but every time I looked at the holes in the wall, I cringed. What could have happened had been playing on a loop in my head.

I'd called in sick to work. It's not like I was lying—I really was sick of my situation. And it didn't make things any better that my life had been thrown into an upheaval.

I tried to busy myself to keep my mind off Phillip's invasion into my life. I didn't have a good feeling about him, and I just knew he was going to cause trouble for me and my family.

I cleaned the entire downstairs, but before I knew it I was back in front of my laptop, trying to dig up more information on the Logans. There was no shortage of pictures and articles about my father. But at every charity event, every major dinner, everywhere . . . he was alone. A few of the articles made mention of the depression his wife had suffered since the abduction of their child, but in public it was just Major rolling solo.

I sighed and closed my laptop just as my husband walked in the front door with a look of exasperation on his face.

"No luck?" I asked, even though I already knew the answer. Malcolm had awakened this morning determined to find a job so we could move.

He shook his head and sat down. "No. Reggie just had to let

two guys go at the garage because business has slowed down. We have to get out of here. Next time we might not be so lucky."

Now would be the perfect time to tell him about Phillip's offer, but the words wouldn't come. Plus, I was unsure how my husband would react, especially now that he seemed desperate to move.

"Are you okay?" he said, finally noticing the expression on my face.

I sighed. "Not really. Phillip came over here."

"Your cousin?"

I couldn't believe the ease with which Malcolm just welcomed these people into our lives.

"Major's nephew." I corrected him.

That caused Malcolm to sit up. "Oh really? What did he want?"

"Well, initially he said he was in the area and just wanted to drop by. I knew that was a lie." I sat down next to my husband. "Basically he came to offer me a check to go away. For fifty grand."

Malcolm frowned. "Go away? As if Major would even let that happen."

"I think Phillip really believes I'm only about the money, which is crazy because he doesn't even know me," I said. "But he tried to give me the whole 'you could have money to move, and you'd get to keep your relationship with your mom' spiel."

Malcolm looked like he was thinking. I just knew he was about to chastise me for kicking Philip out without entertaining his offer.

"I know you probably think I should have taken the money," I said after we sat in momentary silence.

"No," Malcolm replied, "actually, I'm thinking if he was willing to give you fifty thousand to disappear, how much are the Logans going to give you to stay?"

"Malcolm, my life is about more than money," I said, frustrated. I could see how money became an issue for people. It felt like it dominated every conversation with us now.

Malcolm scooted closer to me. "You know I don't mean it like that," he said, taking me into his arms. "You know where my heart is, babe. I'm sorry if it seems like that. I'm just so frustrated raising my child in this place." He pointed toward the bullet hole in the wall. "I can't seem to catch a break."

Before I could reply, my phone rang. I grabbed it off the coffee table.

"It's Major," I said, pressing the Talk button and putting him on speaker. "Hello?"

Panic was in his voice. "Jill, I just heard what happened. Is everybody okay?"

I cut my eyes at Malcolm and when he immediately looked away, I knew he'd called Major. My only question was why.

"Yes," I said, returning to the phone conversation. "We're fine. The neighbors are just into some bad stuff and we got caught in the crossfire."

"My God," he said. "You've got to move. That is utterly ridiculous."

I sighed. I wasn't in the mood to deal with this right now. "Okay, Dad, we can talk about it later."

"What is there to talk about?" he said. "No daughter of mine should be living in a place where she has to dodge bullets." He paused. "Can you and Malcolm be at my Houston office tomorrow?"

"For what?" I asked.

"Just indulge me," he said.

"Fine," I replied. "I'll come but I have to go to work at one p.m., so I can't stay long."

"I will see you then. In the meantime, stay safe!"

When I hung up, my husband was standing in the middle of the floor with a smile.

I didn't return his smile. "Why did you call him?" I asked.

Malcolm shrugged. But I could tell he was nervous about my reaction.

"Babe, I'm sorry," he said. "I just felt like they should know." He paused. "And I was thinking maybe he could help me find a job."

"You asked him that?" I said, stunned that the man who wouldn't ask his own family for anything was putting in requests to my newfound relatives.

"I did," he said defiantly. "It's time out for that prideful stuff. We've got to get our daughter out of this hellhole and the only way we can do that is if he can help me find a job." I rolled my eyes and my husband squeezed me tighter. "This is good, baby," he said. "Real good."

I nodded, but only because I didn't want to argue with him. But something told me that this wasn't about to wrap up in a nice big bow anytime soon.

Chapter 20

My life could be on the verge of changing. Forget that, it could be about to shift completely off its axis.

I could tell that money was still at the forefront of Malcolm's mind. He was so giddy that right about now, I was wishing that I had just decided to go to the attorney's office by myself, but I knew that I needed my husband's support. Besides, the way his mood had instantly changed after Major's call, no way would he have let me come alone.

Plus, my husband had already played out this scenario multiple times. "So, do you think they're going to cut you a check?" he asked as he straightened his tie.

"I have no idea. You heard him. Major just asked us if we could be at their attorney's office at ten a.m. We'll find out when we get there." I placed a pearl earring in, then snatched it right back out. Why was I so concerned with my appearance? I'd spent the past hour trying to find the perfect outfit. I guess I was just on edge.

"God, I hope they do cut you a check," Malcolm said. "It's not like they're going to miss it. They are millionaires."

"You know we're not doing this for the money," I said, turning to him as I tried to hide my agitation.

He stopped securing his tie and looked at me. "Babe, I know that. And I don't mean to make light of this at all. I know this is hard on you." He pulled me to him and put a kiss on my fore-head. "And I am here for you, no matter what." He released me from his grasp and added, "But I can't help but get excited at the thought that maybe we can finally get some financial footing."

I guess I had to give my husband that much. This all had been so much to process that I had never thought about the fact that they really could write me a check today.

"You know, I looked up his net worth," Malcolm said with trepidation.

"Really, Malcolm?"

He shrugged. "Yeah. When you first told me they thought you were their daughter, I looked them up. Major Logan's company is worth fifteen million dollars. Mrs. Logan's family is worth three times that. So he ought to give you a couple hundred thousand. at least. Do you know what we could do with that?" Malcolm said. I could see the cash register ringing up in his head. "And we'd have the money to finish up this app development. I just need about twenty thousand dollars and I could get everything I needed."

"Again, slow your roll," I told him. "Let's not get ahead of our-selves."

"I'm just saying, babe. We need this."

I let out a sigh and said, "Can we just go see what they want and be done?"

He kissed me again and pulled me close. "It's going to be okay, sweetheart. We're going to be okay." I nodded and headed out of our bedroom just as I heard him mumble, "Especially if they give us a check."

Downstairs, Aunt Marilyn was sitting on the sofa, bouncing Destiny on her lap.

"We'll be back in a little bit," I told her.

"Well, your mama is still asleep and Destiny is in good hands," she said.

Malcolm and I kissed our daughter and made our way to the attorney's office.

We were silent on the drive over. I was thinking about what this discovery meant for my life. I'm sure my husband was thinking about what getting some money could mean for us.

Major had us meeting him in his attorney's office in downtown Houston. I was glad because I couldn't imagine the one and a half hour drive to Beaumont with my stomach doing flip flops the way it was.

We were greeted by the receptionist, a perky brunette, who stood and greeted us like we were some fairytale legend that had come to life.

"It is such an honor to meet you," she told me. "Please have a seat. Can I get you anything, water, coffee, soda?"

"No, thank you. We're fine," I said, speaking for my husband as well.

"Okay, it will be just a minute," she said with a smile before darting off.

As Malcolm and I sat in the waiting room, I couldn't help but take in the masculine décor. The place reminded me of leather, tobacco, and liquor.

Malcolm took my hand and squeezed it, instantly calming my nerves. We sat in silence for five minutes, though it actually felt like thirty.

The receptionist reappeared. "You can come back."

We walked down a long hallway, adorned with awards, certificates, and photos of what I assumed were dignitaries. As soon as we entered the room that the receptionist had guided us to, Major stood and greeted us.

"Jill, thank you so much for coming on such short notice." He leaned in and hugged me. "And Malcolm, so good to see you again."

"Hello, Mr. Logan," Malcolm said, shaking his hand.

"None of that Mr. Logan stuff," Major said, waving away his words. "I'm Major . . ." he looked over to me, "and hopefully, one day, Dad."

I wanted to tell him that he was moving way too fast, but I didn't get a chance to, because before I knew it, Elaine was up and throwing her arms around me.

"Alicia, my love!" she sang as she, too, pulled me into her arms. I wanted to ask her not to call me by a name that I didn't know. I also wanted to remind them that they'd just seen me a couple of days ago, since they were acting like I'd just returned from the war.

As I pulled from her embrace, I noticed Phillip sitting over on the sofa up against the wall, his lips pursed together. He didn't bother to speak, so neither did I.

"Please, have a seat." Major motioned toward two wood-backed chairs that were positioned next to him. The door opened and the man that was with him that day in Starbucks walked in.

"Hello, let me formally introduce myself. I'm Vincent Thompson, Attorney-at-Law." He shook my hand, then turned and shook Malcolm's.

"Vince here has been our family attorney for as long as we have needed an attorney." Major smiled.

"Yes, I consider the Logans family, not just clients," he said, taking a seat behind his desk. "I was there when you disappeared and I can tell you they were absolutely heartbroken."

The jovial tone that Elaine had just had disappeared as a thin mist covered her eyes.

"But we aren't going to dwell on the past," Major said. "We have our daughter home now."

I nodded because I didn't know what else to do. "So, what did you want to see us about?" I asked.

Phillip coughed loudly in the background. Major and the attorney ignored him.

"Well, you know, since the test came back positive," Major began, "we have been thinking about how we can build a legacy. And we have so much to give, not just financially, but in love. So we'd love to start by meeting Destiny, our granddaughter."

"We'd love nothing more," Elaine added with a smile.

"That can be arranged." I nodded, looking at Malcolm. He nodded as well. "Maybe we can bring her by this weekend."

"Perfect," Elaine said, the bright smile returning to her eyes. "I can't wait to get to know her. I have so many things I want to do with her. Things that I didn't get to do with you."

I instantly tensed. I hoped that she didn't think that she was going to commandeer our child and duplicate my childhood.

Major must've been reading my body language because he added, "Of course our goal is to get to know all of you, our grand-daughter, and our son-in-law, better."

I nodded again. "We'd like that as well."

"Yes, sir, we would," Malcolm echoed.

Major clapped his hands, signaling a shift in the conversation. "Well, as you might have heard, my business is very lucrative. And one of the things that we have been big on is keeping that business in the family," Major continued.

I raised an eyebrow, wondering where he was going with this conversation. Surely, he wasn't turning his businesses over to a perfect stranger and, blood or not, that's what I was.

"So, I'd like to find a place for you there," he continued.

"I, umm, I work in the healthcare industry," I said.

He smiled. "You actually work at Starbucks."

"And no daughter of ours needs to work at Starbucks," Elaine interjected.

"I'm sure we can find something that you'd like to do," Major said.

I shrugged. "I guess so."

He turned to Malcolm. My husband's eyes were dancing in anticipation. "And I've been doing my homework on you, young man. Seems you're pretty skilled. I'd love for you to join us in our facilities department. I hear you have quite the knack for fixing things. Ideally, I'd love for you to start there and work your way up and learn all aspects of our business."

Malcolm's eyes lit up.

"Of course, it's a good salary," Major said.

"More than we pay anyone that works in facilities," Phillip added from the back.

Again, Major ignored him.

"Yes, sir," Malcolm exclaimed. "I mean, I can give you my résumé." He paused. "But, sir, I'm so much more than a facilities manager. In fact, I'm working on developing a location app to allow people to see things going on wherever they are, and put them with like-minded individuals. It's a combination of FourSquare and Bumble, but safer and more tailored to a person's likes."

"Don't worry. We've done all of our homework. I wouldn't be offering this if I didn't think you were capable," Major said. "And I'd love to hear more about this app. Logan Investments is always looking for ways to diversify our portfolio."

"Wow." Malcolm stood and shook his hand. "I'm honored and yes, yes I'd love to. I can be there tomorrow."

Major laughed. "See, this is why I know you'll do well. Not necessary. You can start next Monday." He handed Malcolm a business card. "This is Barbara Martin, our HR Director, please speak with her. She'll know to expect you and help you get settled." He turned back to me. "I know that you may want to take some more time with Destiny. So whenever you're ready, just let me know."

"Well, thank you," I said, wondering why he couldn't tell us this over the phone.

"Another matter at hand," the attorney interrupted, "is Mr. Logan's distribution of wealth."

That made both me and Malcolm turn our attention back to the front and Phillip grunted his displeasure.

"Mr. Logan would like to make sure you and your family want for nothing," Vincent began. "We are in the process of revamping his will but in the meantime, he'd like to give you and your family this check." Vincent slid a check across the desk to us. Malcolm reached out and grabbed it before I could.

"Now in no way do I want to insult your ability to provide for your family," Major said. "But I worked hard so that my family could live a good life. And you're family."

Malcolm gasped as he looked at the check. "Oh my God," he said, handing it to me.

My eyes zoomed in on the zeroes. All five of them. "Five hundred thousand dollars?" I replied, in shock. Surely, this had to be some kind of mistake.

"That's just seed money for now," Major said, a big grin spread across his face.

"Yes," Vincent added. "Once we get the will taken care of and get some other things worked out, Mr. Logan has said that he would like a large amount of his four hundred million dollar estate to go to you."

"Wh—what?" Both Malcolm and I said at the same time.

"Four hundred? I read that you were worth like five million," Malcolm said.

Major laughed. "You can't believe everything you read on the internet."

"So, you have been researching your meal ticket?" Phillip mumbled from the back.

Malcolm cocked his head, refusing to be intimidated by Phillip's disparaging attitude. "No, I call it doing my homework," he replied.

Major laughed. "I like him. I like him a lot." He shifted his gaze directly at me. "Sweetheart, you're a Logan. Life as you know it is about to change."

I don't know why, but a sickening feeling filled my gut.

Chapter 21

My husband reached over and squeezed my hand again. But this time, I thought it was to calm his own nerves, not mine. The Logans and their attorney had stepped into the conference room next door. I didn't know why, but they asked us to hang on for a second after Phillip muttered something in Major's ear. Malcolm could barely contain his excitement.

"Can you believe this?" Malcolm whispered.

I shook my head simply because I couldn't. How had my life changed so drastically in the span of a week?

"Do you know what we can do with this money?" he said. "Thank you, Jesus." He clutched the check to his chest.

"I don't feel right about this," I said.

"What's not to feel right about? I mean, I understand you're conflicted with all of it but you deserve this." He glanced around the room, then leaned in and lowered his voice. "And at four hundred million, you deserve a whole lot more."

"I know," I sighed.

He sat back upright. "And what I like most of all, and yes, I really appreciate the money, but he's giving me a chance to earn my keep. I want to be able to prove that I'm worthy of being your husband," Malcolm said.

I kissed his hand. "I know you're worthy of being my husband, sweetie. It's just . . ." My words trailed off as the door opened back up and the Logans stepped back in. The jovial disposition had disappeared, replaced by an uneasy aura.

"Thank you both for being so patient," Vincent said. "Before we sign the documents, there is one other small matter that must be addressed." He glanced at the Logans. "Mr. Logan?"

Major looked at me but couldn't open his mouth. He turned to his wife and she pressed her lips together.

"Oh, good grief," Phillip said, stepping in front of them. "As you can imagine, this has all been a shock for my family," Phillip began. "And your kidnapping altered the course of their lives."

I nodded in understanding. I knew if my life had been turned upside down by this revelation, I could only imagine what they were feeling.

"But at least you found her now," Malcolm said as if he was fearful that they were about to change their mind and rip the check from his pocket.

"Yes, we're very glad of that." Elaine finally spoke up. "However, this is a large sum of money that we are giving to you."

"I didn't ask you for this," I felt inclined to say. The last thing I ever wanted was them feeling like they could buy me. Malcolm squeezed my hand and Phillip held up his hand to stop me from talking.

"We know that you did not ask for anything," Major said. "We know that you did not seek us out."

"However," Phillip added, "as you can imagine, as grateful as my aunt and uncle are to have found you, they are not happy about the situation and how it unfolded, and how they have been denied a lifetime of knowing you."

I really didn't know what they expected me to say at this point. So, I just found comfort in my husband's touch.

"So, here's the deal," Phillip said as he began pacing back and forth in front of Vincent's desk. "You are welcome to that money," he said motioning toward Malcolm's jacket, "I'm sure it is burning a hole in your pocket there." I wanted to say something about his dig, but he continued talking. "And my uncle is adamant about the estate and," Phillip seemed like he was taking a deep breath and swallowing a lump in his throat, "and the adjustment to his will. However, there is one stipulation to both the money and the will."

That wiped the smile off of Malcolm's face and caused my ears to perk up.

Phillip seemed to take great pleasure in delivering his next words. "You are to have no more contact with Connie Harrison, the woman who kidnapped you."

The room grew silent until I said, "What?"

Major spoke up. "Our first inclination is to have your kidnapper thrown under the jail, but we understand that she is sickly, and for you—and only for you—we won't press charges."

Phillip handed me another piece of paper. "This document states that upon the cashing of that check and signing of the revised terms of the will, my aunt and uncle would like to begin building a relationship with you. They cannot do that with a constant reminder of the woman who ripped you from their lives."

"This is crazy," I said, my attention directly on Elaine and Major. "You want me to abandon my mother?"

"I am your mother," Elaine said. Gone were all traces of a smile.

Major put his arm around her and squeezed her tight, and she appeared to relax just a bit.

"I am sorry," I said, standing to face them. "I don't mean any disrespect as I know this is hard on all of us. And you very well might have given birth to me but," I choked back my tears, "Connie Harrison is my mother."

"Connie Harrison stole you from me," Elaine shouted, before taking a deep breath and stepping back.

Phillip stepped up. "This is exactly why we need to erase all references to that woman from your life. My aunt is fragile and does not need this stress." I couldn't help but note how he seemed to take great pride in all of this.

"Did you suggest this?" I asked him. "Is this your way of trying to make sure only you can benefit from their wealth?"

He didn't seem fazed by my outburst. Just kept standing there with that stupid smirk on his face.

"Look," he replied, moving in front of Major as if he wanted to send a message about who was really in charge. "All I know is that if you would like the money, then you are to have no more contact with your mother, excuse me, your kidnapper. You're lucky that is the only thing we are doing and not choosing to have your mother arrested."

"Arrested?" I gasped.

"Yes. Thrown under the jail," he said. "Kidnapping is a felony."

My heart sank into my chest. I knew that was a possibility, but I guess I refused to believe that it could actually happen. "My mother is very sick," I said, my voice low.

"Which is why we're having mercy on her, though she had no mercy on my aunt or my uncle," Phillip said, unmoved.

"I can't abandon my mother." The very thought made me sick to my stomach.

"Well, it is the only way this can work," Phillip said, motioning between me and Elaine.

"You know what you can do with your check?" I said, stretching my hand out toward my husband. "Babe, give it here." I was prepared to tear the check up in their faces and tell them to go to hell on my way out the door.

Instead of reaching in his pocket, pulling the check out, and placing it in my hand, my husband took my palm and squeezed it.

"Okay, everyone, this is emotional for us all." Malcolm gently pulled me to him. "Can you give us some time to discuss this?"

"Discuss all you want," Phillip said. The way his smirk crept across his face, I could tell this had all been his idea. "If that check is cashed and you do not cease contact with Connie Harrison, we will have her arrested."

I felt tears well up as I moved toward the door, "Malcolm, let's go."

"Alicia, please understand," Elaine said.

I spun toward her, my sudden movement startling her. "My name is Jill," I snapped. "Jillian Jaye Harrison." My tone caused her to take a step back.

"Okay, I understand that this is difficult," Major said, finally stepping from behind Phillip. "Yes, take all the time you need. It took us this long to find you, we're not going anywhere."

"Jill," Elaine muttered as I headed toward the door. "Please don't be upset. Please understand this from our point of view."

I ignored her and cursed the day that any of them had come into my life.

Chapter 22

I couldn't fight back the tears. I'd been crying all the way home. These people had bogarted their way into my past and now wanted to dictate my future. And they were out of their minds if they thought that my future would be without my mother—no matter what she'd done.

Malcolm was conflicted. I could tell he'd already started spending the money in his head, but at the same time, he wanted to comfort me because he knew I was livid.

"You okay?" he asked once we finally pulled back into our complex.

"No," I said, gazing out at my town home, taking in the stark contrast from the Logan's home. "Those people have a lot of nerve."

Malcolm pulled into a parking space, stopped, and turned to face me. "Sweetheart, I understand that you are angry about their request, but I'm going to play devil's advocate here."

I cut my eyes at him, pursed my lips to let him know I didn't care for him to continue. He didn't care that I didn't care and continued to talk.

"What I want you to do is put yourself in Mrs. Logan's shoes. If someone came along and took Destiny from you, robbed you of watching her take her first step, took away everything. Her first words, kiss, date, prom, graduation, all of that, would you be able to forgive her?"

Of course, the answer to that was a resounding "no," but I couldn't bring myself to utter those words. "I'm not saying that I don't understand their anger," I replied. "But this isn't some hypothetical situation. This is real life. My life."

"And if you one day found Destiny, who had been kidnapped from you," Malcolm continued, "how would you feel if she wanted to continue a relationship with the woman who stole her?"

"Again, I can't speak about 'what ifs,'" I snapped. "This is my life." I huffed and folded my arms across my chest. "So, you agree with them that I should walk away from my mother? Do you hear how crazy that sounds?"

"No, of course I'm not saying that," Malcolm said. "I'm just saying that you have to be respectful and understand where their anger is coming from."

"All you care about is the money," I snapped. "They flash some dollar signs and you're ready to toss my mother to the side."

He bit down on his bottom lip like he was trying to choose his words carefully. When he spoke, his words were slow and measured. "Of course I care about the money, Jill. What kind of husband and father would I be if I didn't? That money will change our lives. Change Destiny's life. And any future children we may have. We talked about having more children but at this rate, we can't afford to. We wanted a big family. This would allow us the opportunity to have that. And you know, as much as I love the thought of having this money," he pulled the check from his jacket pocket, "you know my first priority is your happiness. And if tearing this check up will make you happy, I'll do that. If you don't know anything else, you know that."

I sniffled and wiped the tears that had started trickling down my cheek. "Yes, I know," I muttered.

"So, I'm going to support whatever decision you want," he continued. "But I want you to be realistic. We'd already discussed how we can't afford to keep taking care of your mother as it is. Plus, you'll need to hire an attorney because they will try to prosecute your mother. I don't know what the answer is."

"I'm not walking away from my mother," I said with finality.

He let out a sigh and I could see his mind racing for options. "Maybe you can just tell them you're walking away from her, but not really do it," he finally said.

"I'm not even lying about something like that. It's not happening," I said.

He leaned back in the seat like he was still thinking. "Okay, why don't you go back with a counteroffer?"

"Like what?"

He shrugged. "I don't know. Tell them that they need to pay for your mother to go to a memory care center, or something like that. That way, they will feel like they get her out of the way and it will actually help her, not to mention take a huge burden off of us."

It made me sick to my stomach when he called my mother a burden. I knew that he didn't mean it as harshly as it sounded but it still bothered me. "I don't think they're going to do that. They hate her."

"It's a compromise. Emphasize how sick your mother is and tell them it won't do anyone any good to lock her up. And it will only further the divide between you all. Go back and tell them your offer."

"So my counteroffer is to put my mother in a home?" I asked. Every time that thought entered my mind, I got sick to my stomach.

Malcolm took my hand again. "We'd been talking about it, Jill. We can't physically continue to care for her. Aunt Marilyn is old, she can't do it. It's causing everyone to suffer."

The somersaults in my stomach continued. "So now you're talking like my mother is an inconvenience to everyone."

"The reality is, she would be so much better served in a facility. I've been saying that but we just couldn't afford the best facility. We can now. And if that's your counter, it doesn't even have to come out of our newfound money." He patted his jacket pocket again.

"These people are not going to pay for her to go to a facility." I shook my head. "If they hated my mother enough to demand that I never see her again, I can't imagine them now doing anything to help her."

"Just tell them that you will meet them halfway if they send your mother to a facility. I believe their love for you will override their hatred of her."

My shoulders slumped. As much as I didn't want to do it, I knew my husband was right. "I feel like I'm selling my soul. I can't even think about this right now." I started gathering my purse and jacket. "I need to try and get answers from my mom. I need to understand that first. None of this is making sense to me. Why would she do something like this? I get that the DNA test says that I'm their child, but I'm still praying that it is some big misunderstanding. Maybe there was a mix-up at the hospital."

My husband reached over and gently caressed my face. "You were kidnapped, Jill." It's as if he was hoping his touch would ease the pain of that reality.

"Do you think my mother is just some cold, callous criminal?" I asked, my eyes moist with tears.

Malcolm shook his head. "I don't know. I don't know why. And babe," he took my hand, "I agree that you should get answers. Otherwise, you will stay tormented. I don't think you're going to rest until you know why."

"But how do I get that answer?" I asked.

He snapped his fingers as an idea popped into his head. "You know what? I was reading up on caregiving for dementia patients."

That brought a small smile on my face. It was little things like this that made me appreciate my husband even more. "You are so sweet."

"This is difficult, babe. It really is and I'm just trying to figure out how to make the best of this situation because I know how much this means to you. But the article said that sometimes when you take people back to places where they built a lot of memories, it will jog their memories."

"So what? Go back to the house I grew up in?" I asked. My mother had moved out of my childhood home when I'd started college. Unfortunately, the rent and upkeep just got to be too much, so she'd moved into a small government-subsidized apartment, where she had stayed until we had to move her in with us six months ago. The landlady was someone who had gone to church with my mother and it was my understanding that her son now lived in the house. Maybe if I explained everything, he would let me bring Mama by.

Malcolm shrugged. "It's worth a shot. Take her on one of the days that you think she is pretty lucid, try it and see if you can talk to her and get some answers."

I nodded and then reached in to hug my husband. He'd done what he'd been the master at doing since the day we met—calmed my nerves and given me hope.

Chapter 23

The years had not been kind to my old neighborhood. So much had changed in the ten years since I'd last set foot in Almeda Plaza. Not only was the neighborhood itself dilapidated and run down, the businesses that sat at the front of my childhood neighborhood were now boarded up and closed.

I smiled as I remembered the beauty shop where my mother would bring me to get my hair braided; the record store I used to go to with my friends. The snowball place where we used to get sno cones in all our favorite flavors. The U Tote Em convenience store, where Old Man Waddell used to give us all free candy. He created such a family atmosphere, such a brotherhood in the neighborhood, that no one dared steal from him.

This place would always be home.

Thankfully, the landlady, Mrs. Willis, had put me in touch with her son. When I explained about my mother, he'd been more than happy to let us come visit. I'd texted him to let him know we were on the way and he'd left the key under the mat while he ran a quick errand.

"Where are we going?" my mother asked as we pulled onto Dragonwick Street. She leaned forward and studied the surroundings. "Is this our neighborhood?" she said with a nostalgic smile.

"It is," I replied.

"Oh my God. Look at our house," she exclaimed as I pulled into the driveway of our old home. Obviously, Mrs. Willis's son was taking good care of the place. The grass was freshly cut and colorful plants sat on the porch.

"Do you remember what I used to draw on the driveway all the time?" I asked after we'd stepped out of the car. Like a Mad Lib, I want her to fill in the blanks.

She bit her lip and I could tell she was reaching into the recesses of her mind for the answer.

"No, what?" she asked.

The singsong tone of my own voice reminded me of when I try and get Destiny to understand what I'm saying. "You remember how I would draw pictures of our family?" I said.

"Oh, yeah." She flashed a wide smile. "You would draw these giant stick figures of me, you, and your daddy."

A twinge raced through my heart. "That's right." I sighed. "Okay, let's go in."

"What if someone is living there?"

I swallowed my emotions and said, "Someone does, but I talked to him and he said that we could come visit."

She frowned. "Why don't I live here?"

"Because you can't live alone."

"Then why don't you live here with me?"

"Because I have a family," I said, not wanting to get into the fact that Malcolm and I agreed that we wanted to raise our child in a neighborhood where she would have kids her own age to play with.

"Be careful on that front step," my mother said as we approached the house.

The fact that she remembered that was a promising sign. I stretched over the step that had almost broken my ankle when I was twelve. It looked like it had been fixed, but I was careful anyway.

I got the key from under the mat, put it in the lock, then jim-
mied it until the door opened.

I couldn't believe I hadn't been here in so long. I stepped to
the side and allowed my mother to enter. She slowly went through
the house, touching walls, running her fingers along the counter-
tops, trying to touch the memories of our past.

She studied the stairs as though seeing them for the first time,
even though she'd walked past them several times a day for more
than fifteen years.

"Do you remember when you tumbled down those stairs when
you were seven and scraped your leg, but screamed like you'd
broken it?"

"Oh, yeah," I laughed. "I was a little extra, wasn't I?"

She nodded. "Yes, you were. I haven't lost that memory," she
said with a smile. And then that smile faded as she added, "Yet."

Like my mother, I took my time looking through the house.
Much had changed. The wall between the tiny kitchen and the
formal dining room had come down, creating a contemporary
eating and dining space. The outdated bathroom and a small
closet had merged into a luxurious spa. Some things remained
just as they were in my childhood, though. The tile in the main
floor bathroom was still the ancient, thin, powder blue strips with
fleur-de-lis accents. I wandered back out to the front and over to
the sunny picture window in the living room where I used to listen to my Destiny's Child records on my mother's stereo. I
squinted to block out the new silver-blue paint, trying to make the
room look just as it had two decades ago. The tiny wood-paneled
den held memories of a childhood filled with love.

"Do you remember the time I sat you here and did your hair
for Easter?" she asked as she pointed to the kitchen counter.
"When you wore those pretty pigtails and red yarn ribbons for
the Easter program?"

I nodded, impressed that she remembered such details. "I do. I remember that." I couldn't help but smile. "I'm glad that you do, too."

She kept her smile, though her eyes turned sad. "All of these memories live within me. It's the newer ones that I struggle with."

She continued making her way through the house. I gave her her space, hoping the familiarity would in turn breed answers.

After about fifteen minutes, I said, "Mama, I have some things I'd like you to go through." I reached in the tote bag that I had brought in with me and pulled out a box.

"What is that?" she asked.

"Our picture box," I replied as I set the box on the kitchen table. "Remember, this is where you kept them all?"

"Oh yeah," she said. "I hadn't seen those in years."

I motioned for her to take a seat at the table. Together we sat and went through the pictures in the box. My baptism. My kindergarten graduation. When I lost my first tooth. My high school prom. With each picture my mother turned nostalgic.

"I remember all of these," she said, caressing the photos, her touch speaking volumes on her love.

Before she got too lost in her brain, I pulled out another picture and slid it toward her. "Do you remember this picture, Mama?" I asked.

"Oh my God. Of course I do," she said with a wide smile. "I was eight months pregnant."

I nodded, unsure of how I felt, because if the DNA test was accurate, my mother was boldly lying to my face. And that deception hurt just as much as the thought that I'd been stolen. "It's a beautiful photo," I told her. "You look so happy."

"I was," she said, stroking the picture.

I took a deep breath. "The problem is, Mom," I turned the picture over, "this picture is dated July 1991. I wasn't born until

August of 1993." I watched my mother's face turn up in confusion. I'd seen this picture many times before, but had never paid attention to the date until I began the quest for answers about my past.

"M-maybe the d-date is wrong," my mother stammered. I couldn't tell if she really believed that or if she was covering a lie. That in and of itself made me sad.

"Mother, I need you to tell me the truth. If that's not me you're pregnant with, who is it? Are you even really pregnant?"

"Of course I was pregnant," she snapped. "Do you think I would fake that?"

"I don't know what to think, Mama."

Suddenly, she began fanning herself. "Oh, it's so hot in here. Maybe we should get going. I don't want either of us having a heat stroke." She tried to stand.

"No," I said, grabbing her arm to stop her. I must have startled her because she jumped.

"Please don't yell at me," she said.

I stood so that I was face to face with her. "I'm not yelling, but, Mama, if you ever loved me . . ."

"You know I love you," she said, appalled.

"If you love me," I continued, "I need you to tell me the truth. I told you I met this couple who says that I am their child. They are adamant that you kidnapped me when I was a baby, and I need to know the truth." I stared at my mother, trying to take in every flinch, every twist, everything that might give me a clue to the truth.

"I-I've told you the truth," she stammered again, her eyes wide as she quickly looked away.

I stomped to emphasize my frustration, especially now that I could tell this wasn't a memory issue. My mother was straight up lying. "No you haven't."

My mother was shivering but I couldn't muster the sympathy that always caused me to let complicated issues go.

"I want to know the truth," I demanded. "I have been in contact with them and everything they are saying is adding up. I swear, Mama—"

"You've been in contact with Major?" she asked.

Goosebumps made an instant trek up my arms. "How do you know his name?" I asked. My expression dared her to lie some more.

My mothered stuttered and for a moment, it looked like she was contemplating feigning confusion again. But then her shoulders sank in defeat. "They don't deserve you," she mumbled.

My voice was hoarse, just above a whisper as I placed my hand on her arm and said, "What do you mean, they don't deserve me?"

My mother jerked away from me and walked over to the living room window. She stood with her back to me. "*She* didn't deserve you. That woman. You were supposed to be *my* baby. He and I were supposed to be your parents."

I fell back against the wall. "Oh my God, Mama. What are you saying? Do you know Major Logan?"

My mother let out a sob as she buried her face in her hands. "Can we go home? Please? I can't do this."

"No," I said. "No, we cannot go home. I need answers and I need them now. What these people are saying and what I thought I knew are not adding up." My voice rose several octaves. "And you owe me the truth."

I don't think I'd ever spoken so harshly to my mother. But it was time out for kid-gloved conversations.

"What if I can't remember?" she sniffed. She looked up at me as if she was pleading with me to drop this. That only made me want to know more.

"But you do remember," I told her. I took a step toward her so that we were eye-to-eye. "And I need you to tell me before those memories are gone."

She swallowed her defeat, released a long sigh, then said, "Take me home. I have something for you. It should give you all the answers you need."

I don't know why, but I didn't ask any more questions as I locked the house back up and led my mother back to the car.

Chapter 24

I had come to the park that had once brought me so much joy. The park where my mother used to bring me as a child. She'd push me on the swings or spin me around on the merry-go-round and I'd feel like I was at Six Flags.

Normally, that memory would make me smile. Today, it made me cry. If my mother hadn't done what she'd done, my life could've been filled with trips to the real Six Flags, exotic destinations, and who knows where else. I would've had a completely different past, present, and future.

Now, I could only hope that this faded yellow journal would help me to understand why I had the life I had. When we returned home, my mother had gone straight to her room, retrieved the journal, came back, handed it to me, and said, "This will tell you what you want to know. Go read it someplace private," then she had turned and headed back to her room.

I had fought the urge to read it right there in my living room as I tiptoed back out and headed to the park. I don't know what made me drive all the way back over to our old neighborhood to read this, but I needed to be someplace safe as I read what I now believed was something that was about to turn my world off its axis.

I held the tattered book close to my chest. My heart was racing as I wondered what secrets it would reveal. I didn't see how anything could ever change my view of my mother, but if this held the key to my past and shed a bad light on my mother in the process, I didn't know how I was supposed to react. Internally, I'd crafted all types of explanations to this situation: My mother had inadvertently taken me and by the time she realized it, she couldn't bear to part with me. Or she'd bought me on the black market, Major had sold me to her, or . . . anything. Anything except that she'd stolen me from Major and Elaine Logan.

I eased the book open, closed my eyes, inhaled, released my breath, opened my eyes and started reading.

June 1, 1991
My heart is broken and the tears won't stop. My joyous news didn't go over too well. Of course, I know this isn't an ideal situation. Me being pregnant out of wedlock is not what I wanted, but God doesn't make mistakes. That's exactly what I told him when he freaked out after I broke the news that I was pregnant. He had the nerve to talk about how he was heading to grad school, like that was supposed to make some kind of difference with me deciding to have a child.

I understand his education is important to him. I'm the one that sat and listened to all his dreams of the future—dreams he believed could only be achieved with a college education. I kept him fed, cleaned his house, washed his clothes, did everything I could so all he had to focus on was graduation. I took a year off to work and take care of us. I did it all with no complaint. I was investing in our future.

Now, I can't get his words out of my head. He won't stop talking about how his parents are going to be so angry. Like Aunt Marilyn isn't going to lose her mind. She sent me up here to Wiley to get an education, not a baby. But it is what it is.

Plus, even though I would never tell him this, I don't really care about what his parents think. We are about to be parents ourselves and our focus needs to be on bringing our little girl into the world. If only I could get him to see that.

June 12, 1991

I can't believe this. He has been acting so distant. He didn't meet me after class like normal. And every time I go by his apartment, his roommates claim that he's not there. I know they were lying. I finally cornered him and he ended up telling me that he had been avoiding me on purpose. He said he doesn't want to be a father. And then, he delivered the worst news of my life. He told me he couldn't be a father to our baby because he has a girlfriend. A girlfriend! How is that even possible? Oh, God, I want to die.

June 17, 1991

We talked today. He finally stopped trying to avoid me. He told me he has had a girlfriend back home this whole time. His plan was to just hang with me while he was here at college, but he was always planning on going home to her. How could I not know that? How could I not see that everything he said to me was a lie? He made me feel special. He made me feel loved. He made me believe we had a future. EVERYTHING WITH US WAS A LIE!!!!!

June 19, 1991

He asked me to get an abortion. Take the worst pain ever and multiply it by ten and that's me right now.

June 28, 1991

He moved away. He. Moved. Away. He didn't even say goodbye. He just left. What am I going to do????? What are WE going to do?????

July 3, 1991
I haven't been able to get out of bed. Aunt Marilyn wanted me to come home for the Fourth, but I don't want to leave my bed. My heart is broken in a million little pieces.

July 10, 1991
I got up today. Jazz came by and made me shower and eat. Everybody's worried about me. Aunt Marilyn even called her. But I can't talk to anyone. I don't want to talk to anyone at all—not Aunt Marilyn, not Jazz, no one. I just wish everyone would leave me alone. I feel like I'm losing my mind and I didn't know this much pain was possible. But I have to live. For my baby, I just have to.

August 3, 1991
I felt her move today! It's been so hard to make it each day. Jazz said it would help to keep writing down my feelings (she's the one who bought me this journal in the first place). I barely can function. But it's like my baby girl (I just know it's a girl) is trying to kick some sense into me. Jazz swears it's indigestion or something because she said babies don't kick at five months. But I know my baby. I've bonded with her. That was her way of telling me to be strong. It's hard because I miss him so much. Jazz said I can use her car to go see him. I think that I'm going to do it. Girlfriend or no girlfriend. Maybe if he sees my growing stomach, he'll change his mind. Maybe if he sees our baby, he'll do right by us both.

August 7, 1991
It seemed like a good idea at the time. I guess I shouldn't be surprised, but the visit didn't go well. I went to his mother's house. She didn't even know about me. She didn't know about the baby. So of course, I told her everything, and she told me he's about to get married and I would not be ruining

that. She had the nerve to be mad at me. And she asked me to leave and never contact them again. What kind of mother does that? What kind of woman doesn't want to know her grandchild? Every time I think things can't get worse, they do.

August 11, 1991
I still can't believe he's marrying her. He proposed to her while I'm carrying his child. I'm in this ratty motel, hoping he'll come talk to me. I told his mother to tell him if he didn't come see me, I would show up at his wedding. We (me and the baby) would show up at his wedding, even though I had no idea when it was, I promised her I would be there to introduce our child to her family. I don't want to do something so crazy, but I will. I feel like I'm losing my mind anyway.

August 14, 1991
I'm back in Marshall. He showed up at the motel. But only to echo his mother and ask me to leave him alone. We've been together two years and he wants me to just leave him alone. I hit him over and over, it was so bad, I was so angry that he pushed me trying to get away and I fell against a table. He panicked, but he didn't leave. He was so concerned and I knew that was proof that he loved me. He even took me to the hospital. But once they said I was fine, he left. His mama came to take me back to the motel with a message—Don't ever contact them again or they would get the most expensive lawyers they could afford, sue me and take my baby. Driving home was so hard, I cried the whole way. I almost ran into an 18-wheeler. For a moment, I wished that I had.

October 7, 1991
I had planned to use this journal to document my journey of bringing my baby into this world. I've been MIA because . . . there is no longer a baby. Two weeks before my baby was due,

my placenta completely detached from my uterus, killing my baby within minutes. It was something called a placental abruption. I had no risk factors and had never even heard of that. They told me it was most likely from my high-blood pressure (because I stayed stressed out) and that fall when he pushed me down. I started bleeding internally. They told me my baby died in my womb. And then, my water broke and the contractions started. So I had to give birth and I brought my dead, five-pound, eight-ounce baby girl into the world. The whole time I prayed to hear her cry, that maybe the doctors had gotten it wrong. They hadn't, they brought her to me, wrapped in a blanket. She looked like she was sleeping. And even with no breath in her body, I loved her with every breath in mine. They had to end up prying her body from my arms. I just kept crying and asking what kind of God allows a child to grow in your body for 37 weeks only to take her from you????

Then, as if God wanted to drive a stake through my heart, the doctor delivered more devastating news . . . .because of the internal bleeding, they had to do a complete hysterectomy and I will never be able to have kids. I thought the pain of losing him was bad. Nothing compares to this. Nothing compares to losing your child and your future children in one sweep.

I had to call information to get his number and it took me some time to catch him, but when I did, I just wanted him to comfort me. I wanted him to come so I could bury our baby. I needed his comfort. He sounded relieved that our baby died, then had the nerve to throw my words in my face and tell me "God doesn't make mistakes." I never thought I could hate someone but I hate him with everything in me.

I will bury my baby alone.

I stopped reading when I noticed that a tear had slipped from my eye and onto the paper. My poor mother. I flipped a page and read more entries. Each one tore my heart more than the last.

Over the next year, my mother seemed to spiral out of control into a deep, dark depression that tore at my soul. Every tragic word pierced my heart.

But it was when I got to an entry that said September 9, 1993 that I stopped. I remember that date clearly because it was the day before I was stolen. The words were pressed into the page like she was writing them in extreme anger. My heart raced as I continued reading.

September 9, 1993
So he just gets to go and create a new life? My life is all but over. I've been unable to function, dropped out of school. I have no friends, Aunt Marilyn is worried sick. I had to spend weeks in a mental hospital and he gets to live happily ever after??? I don't think so. She doesn't deserve him and she doesn't deserve a baby. I followed them yesterday and saw them shopping for pink clothes like they're just this big happy family. She might have gotten my man, but she will not raise a daughter that was supposed to be mine.

I frantically turned the page. Then the next page. Then the next. My heart sank as I realized that was the last entry from my mother and it sent a cold chill through my spine.

Chapter 25

"*One day, your mother will come.*"
"*They're going to be really mad.*"
"*They're going to want you back.*"

My mother's words were forefront in my mind. I'd brushed them off as gibberish at the time . . . when all along it was foreshadowing of a truth my mother had buried all my life.

I was not my mother's child.

I was a stolen daughter.

Those words had engulfed me as I sat through dinner like a zombie last night after I returned from the park. My mother, feigning a headache, had stayed in her room. Every time I went in and tried to talk to her, she was asleep. Or acting like she was asleep.

Malcolm had tried to comfort me, but even his touch could bring me no solace after this revelation. I was angry at the lie that had been my life. Angry that when I woke my mother up and pushed her for answers, she did nothing but cry, apologize, and cry some more. I'd finally given up and gone and cried myself to sleep.

I don't even know how I made it through the night. But this morning, I'd gotten up, begged my Aunt Marilyn to come over, taken Destiny to the sitter's, and given my biological mother the one thing she'd been requesting since we'd met—one-on-one time.

And now, as I sat at lunch across from the woman who had carried me in her womb for nine months, my mother's words continued raging in my head.

"One day they'll want you back."

This woman had carried me inside her.

And she was a perfect stranger.

I know that some part of me should have taken the first step, tried to break the ice as we sat here at Lucille's Restaurant in Southwest Houston. But I didn't know what to say to her.

Nervousness was written all over Elaine Logan's face and I could tell she was trying to keep her emotions in check. It was obvious that she was thrilled to be here, but she also seemed cautious in her approach. I'll admit, I wanted to know more about her. About this new, *white* side of my family.

"Thank you for agreeing to have lunch with me," she said after the waiter had delivered our salads. She had been here when I arrived. And I guessed that she was extremely nervous because the waiter was removing one Martini glass and setting another one down when I approached the table.

"You have no idea how much it means to me to have this one-on-one time with you," she continued.

I nodded, unsure of how I should reply.

"I know that you are a little disturbed with us because of the demand we made in regard to the woman who stole you." That caused me to tense up and she immediately reached for my hands. "I'm so sorry. It wasn't my idea, but I can't say I'm totally opposed to it." She squeezed my hands, then released them. "I just missed so much with you."

I heard my husband's words in my head. *"What if someone had taken Destiny?"* That thought caused me to take a deep breath, then try to relax . . . to try and empathize with what this woman was feeling.

"I know you hate her," I said.

Elaine didn't flinch as she said, "I do and I can't even pretend that I don't. And I pray every day for God to remove this hatred from my heart. I have hated the person who took you for so long that I don't know how *not* to. I don't understand why she did what she did. I don't know if I ever will."

I did wonder if she knew about my mother and Major. If she knew that my mother had stalked her, obsessed over her. The thought of a lifetime of unanswered questions pierced my soul and I was overcome with sympathy.

Even still, as grateful as I was that this woman had given me life, my love was with the woman who had helped me live. I debated trying to explain the state of mind my mother was in, but decided against it. Nothing could ever justify what my mother had done when she took me, so there was no use in trying. Plus, I didn't ever want to give them anything to use against her.

"All I do know," I said, trying to reason with her, "is that I was raised in love."

"We would have loved you, too," she said.

"I understand that," I replied. "It's just, I have no control over what *would* have been. All I can do is talk about what *was*."

She nodded in understanding, then took a sip of the martini she'd ordered. She savored it like it was liquid courage.

Finally, she said, "When I found out I was pregnant with you, your father and I weren't actually married yet." She set her drink down. "I was mortified because of my parents. They already had an issue because your father was black. My family isn't exactly progressive," she added. "I knew that my parents would go crazy. And then your dad, being the man that he is, stepped up to the plate. He said they might have a problem with me being pregnant by my boyfriend, but they wouldn't have a problem with me being pregnant by my husband. So, while you were still fresh in my womb, we had a small wedding. His parents had actually been planning this huge wedding, but we convinced them to move the date up and do something smaller. And that was the second happiest day of my life. The first was the day I gave birth to you. When the doctor set you on my chest, I immediately started thinking of all the things we would do to make you happy." She choked back a sob, composed herself and continued. "I wanted to spend a lifetime making you happy. I knew it would be a challenge, raising a mixed-race child. But your father and I were ready. The day that you came up missing was the worst day of my life."

"What happened?" I asked, grateful for the opportunity to learn a little about my past. I didn't lose sight of how he was ready for her child, but not my mother's.

Elaine took her napkin and dabbed at her eyes. "It was only my second time taking you out. I was very protective. I went shopping, then to the park." She managed a convoluted laugh. "Funny thing is, you probably had no idea where you even were. You couldn't have been but about two months old. I went to the park and I walked around with you and you pretty much slept the entire time. Some older woman with gray hair sat next to me. She talked a little bit. One of the sweetest women I'd ever met. I never felt threatened. Of course, we later learned the gray hair was a wig and she was in a disguise. She marveled over you, then went back to reading her book. She told me you were the same age as her daughter. My sister and some friends arrived. They all doted over you then we just started chatting and taking pictures. I looked away at one point and you and the woman were gone."

"So, you turned your back on a two-month-old?" I asked. I couldn't imagine ever turning my back on Destiny.

"I have not forgiven myself ever since," she said. "Your father never blamed me, but he didn't have to. I blamed myself. I've never worked since then. And I'm a shell of my former self. Living without you was akin to living without my heart. Over the years, I often wondered what you would look like. I had recurring dreams of holding you, playing with you. Every time I saw a child your age, I studied their face, hoping it would be you. We plastered posters all over the place. Put up a two hundred and fifty thousand dollar reward for your recovery, even appeared on "America's Most Wanted," and conducted a search across multiple countries. But even with all our money, we kept turning up nothing."

Tears sprang to my eyes.

She continued, "So you have to forgive me if I can't forgive the woman who stole you and altered the course of my life."

I paused, weighing my next words. Finally, I said, "I don't know if you remember, but I told you that my mother is sick . . ."

She slammed her palm on the table, causing me to jump. "I'm your mother." Then she caught herself. "Sorry. I'm so, so sorry." She sipped her drink again like the liquid courage helped to calm her down. "I need you to understand what it does to me when you refer to her as your mother. The only reason she is that to you is because she stole my daughter."

I didn't know what this woman wanted me to say. Connie Harrison was my mother. It didn't matter how she got to be my mother. She was my mother.

"Well, she has early-onset dementia now." And then I don't know why I felt compelled to add the lie, "She doesn't even remember what happened."

"Oh, isn't that convenient?" Elaine chuckled. "But God has a way of getting his own revenge. She snatched away my memories and God took hers."

It must have been the way I pursed my lips that caused Elaine to say, "You know what? I am so sorry. Again. This is all just so difficult for me. Let's talk about something else. Tell me about Destiny. My granddaughter."

That made me smile. I could easily have that conversation. I relaxed as I began to fill her in on all the wonderful things about my baby girl.

Chapter 26

It was my father's turn. I'd gotten insight from Elaine. Now, it was time to hear my father's side.

Short of his joy in finding me, he and I had not talked about my abduction. And it was time that we did. I especially wanted to know how he could hurt my mother the way she'd written about in my journal.

He'd never said anything about my mother, but I couldn't imagine that he'd spent all of that money hiring private investigators to track me down, but hadn't figured out who the woman was who'd kidnapped me.

That's why, immediately after I'd left Elaine yesterday, I'd called my father and asked to meet with him. Of course, he'd been all too eager.

So now, I was sitting in his office, directly across from him. I had greeted him, then handed him my mother's journal.

"What's this?" he asked.

"Just read it, please. It explains a lot. I've marked where I'd like you to start."

Though he seemed confused, he took the book.

I studied him as he read. His hazel eyes matched mine. Our skin color could blend seamlessly. A visual test confirmed what the DNA had already told us.

I remember how I used to stare at photos of Al Harrison (or whoever the man was in the picture my mother kept on our mantel). I would study him, searching for his face, looking for any hint of resemblance to mine. I never found any and now I knew why.

At some point, I needed to know more about the man my mother said was my father. Who was he? Was he some figment of her imagination? The one thing that I did know, though. The man in front of me was real. And right about now, I needed to understand what kind of man would leave his pregnant girlfriend.

I continued watching him as he read. Yes, I probably shouldn't have allowed him to read my mother's innermost thoughts, but I hoped that if he could see the person she had spiraled into, the pain that he had played a part in causing, he would have mercy on my mother. He wouldn't try to make me cut her off. He wouldn't try to send her to jail.

"Wow," he said. I waited patiently as he read. When he finally looked up me fifteen minutes later, a mist covered his eyes. "I-I had no idea she was . . ."

"Spiraling out of control like that?" I said, finishing his sentence.

When my father looked up at me, he struggled to find his words. "I don't know what to say," he said.

"Did you ever love my mother?" I asked.

He shook his head and shrugged. "I don't know. I mean, I liked her a lot. We were young. She was fun. But I told her time and time again that I didn't want anything serious."

"Well, obviously she was serious," I said. "And she obviously thought the two of you had a future."

He glanced back down at the journal. "Oh my God. I just never knew."

My glare tried to pierce him, to see if he was telling the truth. Finally, I said, "When I was abducted, did it ever dawn on you to look at her?"

"No," he said. "I hadn't heard from your mother in a year.

Why would it dawn on me to look at her? We were in Beaumont. She was still in Marshall as far as I knew. Plus, the description of the woman that Elaine gave police was an older, dark-skinned overweight woman."

I thought of my mother's caramel skin and couldn't help but say, "Maybe to Elaine, my mother was dark-skinned."

He shook his head again. "This just makes no sense to me. I never even thought about . . ." His words trailed off and I could tell he was in shock.

My mother must've worn padding, a wig, glasses, the works. She'd proven she was a master at costumes. With the state she was in, nothing that she did surprised me now.

"So, you just left college and never talked to her again?"

"I did a couple of times when she came to Beaumont. But I told her I was getting married. Then, after she lost the baby . . ." His words trailed off again.

"You saw that as a blessing?" I asked.

He lowered his head in shame. "I wish I could say that I didn't, but I truly felt like it was God's way of working everything out. I was twenty-two years old."

"Did you really ask her to get an abortion?"

He nodded. "I did and I have lived with that guilt forever. Even though it didn't happen that way, just the fact that I had even asked her to do something like that tore me apart inside for the longest time. It was a guilt that I've lived with. I wasn't raised like that. I was just young and dumb and panicked. After she lost the baby, I saw that as my way to make a clean break. I had no idea that it had destroyed her like this." He ran his fingers over the book and from the look on his face, he was genuinely remorseful.

Pain filled my heart again as I thought of what my mother had gone through. "Well, it had, especially when she learned that she could never have children. And she blamed you for the fall that killed her baby and damaged her womb."

"I never touched her," he said. "I mean, she was attacking me and when I tried to push her off of me, she fell. But I thought she was fine because she got up and walked away. And then she left and I didn't hear from her again until she called to tell me that she'd lost the baby."

"And you just let her go through that alone?"

Shame filled his face and my heart hurt all over again thinking of my mother going through that tragedy alone.

"Well, she didn't just disappear. Apparently, she stalked you and she knew everything about you and your wife," I said.

He ran his hand over his head. "I don't believe this."

"Believe it," I replied.

He reread a few passages. "So, she just came down here and took you?" I could see the wheels spinning in his head. As if he were mad at himself that it never dawned on him that my mother was behind my disappearance.

"I think in her mind she was rationalizing that I belonged to her."

"Oh my God," was all he could mumble again. "I wasn't trying to hurt her. I was just hanging out with her while I was at school. I knew that she loved me and in a way, I loved her. But never in the way she wanted. And I knew that she was upset when she came to see me in Beaumont, but I thought it was just because she was pregnant. She told me she was seeing someone else right before she lost the baby and I just assumed he was there for her."

"Or maybe you just wanted to absolve yourself," I replied.

I expected him to dispute that, but he simply said, "You're probably right." His shoulders rose, then fell. "I never even thought that she was capable of something like that."

I didn't know what else to say to him. My emotions were all over the place. Nothing could justify what my mother had done. But how much could one woman be expected to endure before she snapped?

"What did your mother have to say about all of this?" he asked.

I stared at him pointedly. "I'm sure your high-powered attorneys that tracked me down have told you the state my mother is in. She has dementia. I can't get her to say much of anything."

He seemed stunned. "Honestly, my focus was on finding you, not finding out who took you. I didn't get a lot of info on your mother because once I located you, that's all I cared about. But the investigators did tell me her name was Connie Harrison. That's why I had no idea."

"So you mean to tell me when they told you her name, even if she was no longer going by her maiden name, you never put two and two together?"

"No! That's just it. I don't know a Connie Harrison. Your mother's real name is Virginia Payne, so I never made the connection," my father said.

My eyes widened in shock. "Virginia Payne? You're mistaken. My mother's name is Connie Harrison."

My father looked confused. "No, her name is Virginia Payne. At least that's what she was in college."

I don't know why, but a memory of creditors calling our house looking for Ms. Payne filled my head.

I remembered it because my mother always had such a fit, yelling at the bill collector, that they were mistaken and had the wrong number.

I felt sick to my stomach. Even my name was a lie.

My father shook off his shock. "Do you think she really doesn't remember, or do you think she doesn't *want* to remember?" he asked.

"I don't know," I said. The tears I had been holding inside finally escaped. My father stood and came over and held me in his arms.

"I am so sorry. So, so sorry," he said, as he hugged me. "I never knew Virginia had lost it like th—"

He stopped midsentence and I followed his gaze toward the door. There, Elaine stood in the doorway. Both of us looked shocked, unsure of how much she'd heard.

"Virginia? The woman you cheated on me with in school? That's who stole my child?" she asked in disbelief. In that moment, I knew that any progress I'd made at lunch with her the other day was out the window. She wouldn't rest until my mother paid for her crime.

"Sweetheart." My father released me and stretched his arms out to her. "I had no idea."

She jerked away from his reach. "My life was ruined over some girl you were cheating on me with while you were away at college?"

"Sweetheart," he repeated.

"Don't sweetheart me!" she screamed. "You robbed me of my child. Both of you! She kidnapped my baby as some vendetta because you were a liar and a cheat. Are you kidding me?" Her face had turned red with anger and she trembled as she spoke. "I want that bitch arrested. I don't care if she's on her deathbed, I want her under the jail!"

That caused me to take a step toward her. "Mrs. Logan—"

"I'm not Mrs. Logan! I'm your damn mother," she screamed. She used both hands to push Major with a force that belied her small frame. "My life was ruined because you played with the wrong woman's heart."

I wanted to say something—anything—to get her to calm down because I saw veins popping out of her temples.

Her outburst shocked me into momentary silence. But I inhaled and said, "I understand you're upset but—"

"No, you don't understand anything," she said, cutting me off again. "Until someone has ripped your child out of your life, you can't possibly understand! But you're about to feel my pain." She spun around to face her husband. "You're disgusting." She whipped her head back in my direction. "Cut her off or she goes to jail. You let me—your real mother—know what you decide. I expect to hear from you tomorrow or the police will be there to pick up your mother the day after tomorrow."

With that, she spun and stomped out of his office.

Chapter 27

It felt like someone was playing a cruel game on me. In one hand was the answer to all my family's financial problems. A life of wealth that was rightfully mine. But in the other, was something that was priceless—a woman who had cared for me, loved me, raised me.

"But she stole you."

The words of my husband rang in my head. He and Cynthia had been up all night consoling me after that meeting with Major. Mama had been upstairs asleep when I'd gotten home. I wanted to go immediately charge her up, ask her to explain her lies—but Malcolm and Cynthia had convinced me that I needed to calm down first.

We went out at my complex and sat by the pool, that had it not been a cool night, would've been a beacon for mosquitos with its brown, dirty water.

They let me cry. They let me vent and then they got real with me.

My mother was a liar.

A liar, a thief, and a kidnapper.

The reality of that hit me in the stomach like a sledgehammer.

My mother was a criminal. And now she was about to pay for her crime.

By no means was I trying to make her pay, but, as she used to say when I was a little girl, "The chickens had come home to roost." My mother was going to have to pay for her crimes either by me cutting her off or actual charges being filed against her. It was a no-win situation for me and her.

The thought of my mother in prison in her frail state sent my stomach into knots. While I understood Mrs. Logan's issue, the reality was that my mother was sick and prison would kill her.

But so would me abandoning her. Not that I even wanted to. It hurt like hell that she was a kidnapper. And a liar.

But she was still my mother.

"So, what are you going to do?" Cynthia asked me, breaking me from my conflicted thoughts.

"I don't have a choice," I sniffed.

"It's going to hurt either way, but you know that your mother loves you," Malcolm assured me. He was sitting next to me on the pool lounging chair. Usually, his presence was comforting when I was stressed but right now, it wasn't helping at all.

"That's one thing I don't doubt but it doesn't make it right what she did," I replied.

"It doesn't," Cynthia said, her voice soothing. "I just want you to do what's going to give you peace."

I leaned back in the pool chair and weighed my options. They were limited.

"I don't have much choice. I'm angry at my mother but not angry enough to lock her away in some home," I balked. "But if I don't, these people are going to make sure she goes to jail."

"What if they do press charges? Like you say, your mom is sick. They wouldn't put her in prison, would they?" Cynthia asked.

I'd played that scenario out in my head as well. "With all the money the Logans have, I wouldn't be surprised if they made sure she got the maximum penalty."

"Yeah. All that money," Cynthia said. "And then, to think about all the money you'd have to spend trying to fight them."

"Money I don't have," I added.

"Dang, I don't know what you should do because that's your money. You're entitled to that."

"But a few weeks ago, I didn't know anything about it. So what if I just went back to pretending I didn't?" I said.

I could feel my husband tense up. Even though I hadn't given him the go ahead to cash the check, Malcolm was already spending our newfound wealth in his head. Just this morning, he talked about how he couldn't wait until he could hire some additional developers to help him work out some of the kinks in his app. I knew that giving the check back and finding money to fight criminal charges was an option he didn't want to even consider.

"I'm going to go to Mrs. Baker's and get Destiny," Malcolm said before leaving us to ourselves. He flashed a look at Cynthia like he was hoping she'd convince me to come to my senses.

After he was gone, Cynthia shifted in the lounge chair so that she was directly facing me. "Let me ask you a question, do you have money to get your mother an attorney?"

"No," I said, solemnly.

"Do you have money for a divorce attorney?" Cynthia's eyes went toward the walkway where Malcolm had just disappeared. "Because I can tell you now, this is going to take a toll on your marriage. Malcolm can say that he supports you, and I believe that he is supportive, but this one will hurt. He's on the cusp of realizing his dream and you're saying not only can he not do that, but he's going to need to find money to hire a criminal attorney for your mother."

"Malcolm would never put his mother in a home. He would never turn his back on his mother, so I don't know why he expects me to," I protested.

"Well, like you once told me, you can't talk on hypotheticals. The reality is, you guys are faced with life-changing money. A life-changing opportunity. And there will be some resentment from him if you walk away from that. He's a good guy so he'll try his best not to show it, but it will be festering underneath."

"That's so wrong," I said. "And I hate that I'm in this position."

"I understand that," Cynthia replied. "All I can tell you is that you're going to have to make a decision soon."

"Yeah, Mrs. Logan said she wants an answer tomorrow."

Cynthia put her hands over mine. "At least they offered to pay for the home. Look at the small blessings."

I nodded. That was a good thing Major had done. He'd called when I was on my way home and told me that he would indeed pay for my mother to go to one of the top memory care facilities. Of course, his wife didn't know anything about it, but he said he wanted to make sure my mother had the best care. And while he hated going behind his wife's back, he would do whatever it took to make things right and that meant making sure my mother had the best care.

"I guess that is a bright spot, isn't it?" I sighed.

"Yeah, it's not like you'd have to put your mother in some dump now. And honestly, that facility may be the best thing anyway. You're young. You have a daughter. You haven't been focusing on Destiny. This money could change Destiny's life. Give her a better life. Get her out of that neighborhood. You guys could have more kids like you want. You're not in a position to be a caregiver, financially or physically," Cynthia said.

I sighed. My best friend was right. I knew I didn't have any other choice. Major's offer was the only option I had. Now, I just had to muster up the strength to tell my mother.

Chapter 28

"So, you're not going to say anything to me?" I stood in the doorway to my mother's room as she stuffed the last of her belongings in a duffel bag. She hadn't even bothered to fold them up, which was a big deal for my obsessively meticulous mother. She didn't say a word as she walked over, pushed all of the toiletries off of her dresser and into a tote bag.

"Mama?" I repeated.

"Oh, am I still your mother?" she said, not bothering to look up.

I swallowed the lump in my throat and fought hard not to cry. When I had woken her up this morning, I'd actually prayed that she'd be in one of her confused states, so she wouldn't be aware that I was moving her into a facility. Major had worked magic—making some calls and before the sun set on yesterday, had found a place for her to go. A place that, in my world just a few weeks ago, would've been unimaginable.

"I can't take care of you anymore," I said. I didn't have the heart to tell her that the Logans wanted her in jail, but it looked like that was the only way she would understand why I was making this decision.

She stopped packing and stared at me, her eyes filled with tears. "I am sick," she said.

"I know you are, Mama," I replied, struggling to fight back tears of my own.

She resumed packing. "But you don't care. Every cold, every sniffle, every bruised knee, everything that's ever ailed you. I've been there. I would have never tossed you away," she said. She stomped over to her closet, snatched a few pair of shoes out, then flung them into the bag.

"Mama . . ."

"And you're a liar, too," she added, cutting me off. "You said that you'd never leave me."

If this didn't hurt so much as it was, I would've addressed the audacity of her calling me a liar. "Mama, I don't have a choice," I blurted.

She stopped packing and stared as tears trickled down her cheeks. "Yes, you do. You and Malcolm just don't want to be bothered with me anymore," she cried.

"Yes, this is difficult for all of us," I admitted. "But that's not the only reason."

She folded her arms in defiance. "Then help me understand why you're doing this. I have been there your entire life, and these people come along and just like that," she snapped her fingers, "you toss me aside."

I was determined not to fall into her sympathy web. My mother had to answer for her transgressions. I stood erect as I said. "I belong to Major and Elaine Logan. You stole me from them." I reached in my bag, pulled out her journal and shook it at her. "You told me I would find answers here, but I really just found more questions. How could you just kidnap me?"

She snatched the book away and held it to her chest. "I don't say anything about a kidnapping in here."

"You don't. But you talk about losing your child. And though you never write his name, I know that the man you're talking about is Major Logan. And the fury that you felt for him is evident."

My mother sobbed and started shaking her head as she plopped down on the bed. "No . . . wait, I can't remember any of this."

Today, for once, I knew my mother was using her illness as a crutch. "No, Mama," I told her. "Do not do that. You are lucid. Yes, you are sick, but today you're in your right mind enough to give me some answers."

It seemed like an eternity as she sat there. Finally, in a soft voice, she held her head up and said, "You were supposed to be mine."

"But I wasn't," I cried. I knew it, but hearing her admit it almost crushed my insides. "You took everything from me. My life was a lie."

She had no words as she just sat there, staring at me, blinking back the truth of her deception.

"Who is Virginia Payne?" I asked.

She stood and turned her back to me.

"Answer me!" I screamed.

She turned back around and her shoulders slumped as she said, "Me. I'm Virginia Payne. I took on Aunt Marilyn's name after you were born."

I felt like the wind was being knocked from me. "Are you kidding me? You stole me, crafted this elaborate lie, and denied me a life that could've changed my existence."

"So, that's what this is about? You're mad because you grew up with me and didn't grow up rich?" She had the nerve to sound angry. "Be careful what you wish for, baby girl. Money is not the root of all happiness." She wagged her finger at me.

"You're missing the point." I exhaled an exasperated breath. "It's not about the money!"

She started zipping her duffel. "It's always about the money. You think I don't know that you guys are using my social security check? You think I don't see the financial bind that you guys are in? You talk about me being a burden, but my check helps around here, too. It's all about the money. And now, you're tossing me away because you have a better offer."

It was useless to try to address that and her defiant attitude was only going to make things worse so I decided to tell her the truth. "Elaine wants you to pay for your crime."

"Oh, now you're on a first name basis with her?" she balked.

I couldn't help but scoff at the audacity of my mother getting mad at the woman she stole me from.

"That woman didn't deserve you," my mother said, her anger rising. "That woman neglected you every time I saw her. She was too busy primping around. You were something on her to-do list."

"That was not your call to make," I said.

"I deserved you!" she shouted. "You were mine. You were supposed to be mine and Major's baby."

"But I wasn't, Mama."

My mother started sobbing again. "He wanted my baby to die. He *willed* my baby to die and then he turned around and had a baby with her. You tell me how that's fair," she cried.

I resisted the urge to go to her, to comfort her. "Life isn't fair, Mama. And it didn't give you the right to just take me."

"You read my journal. I felt like my life was out of my control," she said. "I drove down from Marshall to Beaumont with my mind on autopilot. I had no intention of abducting their child."

"Then how did you end up taking me?" I asked.

The defiance returned as she wiped away her tears. "I saw an opportunity and I took it. All I remember is, I was speed walking away from the park, thinking that at any minute someone could grab my arm and say, 'What do you have in the bag?'"

"You stuffed me in a bag?" I asked.

"I did what I had to do."

"I don't believe this," I replied.

"Did I not give you the best life?" she asked.

"You did." I sighed, exhausted by this revelation. "I'm not taking any of that away, but it wasn't my life. I don't know any of my family. My whole past was made up. I can't help but think of all the lies you told me. Is my daddy even real?" I could tell by the look on her face that Al Harrison was a figment of her imagination.

"Who was the man in the picture? The man I thought was my father my entire life?" I asked, the muscle that was my heart feeling like it was being twisted inside out. "You claimed I was named after his mother. Who is he?"

I wanted to scream when she shrugged nonchalantly and said, "He came with the frame."

"Wow," I said, trembling with a mixture of fury and sadness. The tears that had been trickling down my cheeks turned into a full-fledged stream. Everything was a lie. My chest heaved as I struggled to contain my emotions.

"All I wanted was someone to love," she said. "It wasn't fair that I didn't have anyone."

"Don't you understand?" I said. "You can't just steal someone else's child because you wanted someone to love."

"I didn't steal you. I saved you," she said, matter-of-factly. "What is wrong with that?"

"What's wrong?" I screamed, causing her to jump. I inhaled, exhaled, then softened my tone. "Mama, the Logans want you in jail. What you did is a crime. You could be sent away for a very long time."

That seemed to resonate with her because she sat up, erect, her defiance now replaced with fear.

"I can't go to jail. I-I'm sick."

"The jails are full of sick people." I sighed. "The Logans are naturally livid. But I've gotten them to agree that you could go into a medical facility. That's where I'm taking you."

Of course I left off the part about ceasing all contact, because as angry as I was right now, I didn't see how I would ever be able to do that and there was no need to get her all worked up.

And then she said. "If you put me in a home, then you're dead to me," before she resumed packing.

I just stared at her. "You're the one wrong in all this and yet, you make ultimatums to me?"

She glared at me; her lips pursed. I glared right back. Malcolm stuck his head in the door, interrupting our staredown. "Are you ladies ready to go?" he asked.

My mother gave me a so-what-are-you-going-to-do look. I wiped my tears, looked at my husband and said, "Yes, we are."

Chapter 29

If I thought Major and Elaine's home was massive, I hadn't seen anything yet.

"Wow. So, you own all of this?" I said after completing the tour of Logan Industries. My father apparently had taken a loan from Elaine's father and flipped it into a multi-million-dollar industry. *No wonder he chose her over my mother,* I thought. I pushed aside those thoughts and turned my attention back to the enthusiastic tour that he was wrapping up.

We were standing on a balcony overlooking the massive first floor.

Major pointed to an area in the back. "And so, if you look down in that section, you'll see that we have workers. They are putting the final touches on garments before they head out to the vendors. I am proud to say that *Forbes* ranked us as one of the top ten places to work in the country."

"Wow," I said for what felt like the hundredth time. The pride that he felt in his company was evident as his chest was puffed out with pride.

Malcolm had gone on the first part of the tour with us but he was now off in human resources setting up all his paperwork to begin his job. I could not believe that my husband was about to be making six figures. He'd gone from barely five to six figures with the discovery of my bloodline.

"So, Jill we haven't really had a chance to talk about all of this," Major said once we were sitting back in his office. "How do you feel about everything?"

I hadn't talked to Elaine but I did call Major and tell him that we'd checked my mother into the memory care facility. He'd been sympathetic, though he asked no further questions. But he'd wasted no time in getting Malcolm on board to work. So less than forty-eight hours after I'd put my mother in a home, my husband was poised to begin a new life.

"I'm feeling overwhelmed," I said, glancing around his massive office overlooking the city. My eyes stopped on a baby photo of me sitting on the side of his computer screen. I wondered if he'd just put that there or had it always been there. "As you can imagine, two weeks ago our lives were completely different," I continued. "I can't believe you want us to be a part of all of this."

Major smiled. "Well there's no purpose building all of this if I have no one to leave it to."

"Well, you do have Phillip."

He laughed. I couldn't make out the expression on his face. "Phillip is . . . Phillip. But I have more than enough to go around. And what I love most about Malcolm is that he doesn't have his hand out. He wants to work for the things that he gets."

That made me smile. "Yes, that is a quality about him that I really love and he has been so enthusiastic about starting here. But his dream is to work in app development. He's really good and I think his app could be huge, but it's been a struggle to try and support that dream and survive day to day."

"Yes, he told me about that. And I'm going to see what I can do to help him out."

I stared at my father. "Why are you doing all of this?"

"Because you're my daughter," he replied. "And these are things I would have done all your life, had you been in my life."

I nodded my understanding and pushed back "what could've been" thoughts. I didn't need any more reasons to be getting angry with my mother. The ride to her facility had been heartbreaking enough. But then, when she refused to tell me goodbye, I didn't even know how to react. "Well this definitely has changed things for us."

"Have you decided to cash the check?" he said. "I only ask since you did put your mother in the facility."

I knew that Malcolm was itching to cash it. But cashing it meant that I would have to cut off my mother and that wasn't happening so I made him hold onto it. I'd considered lying, but I felt like even though my life was a lie, lying about cutting off my mother was a betrayal of the highest degree.

"Look, I understand that you aren't on board with the demands," my father said when I didn't say anything. "And trust me, if there was another way we'd explore it, but my wife is adamant about that. As you can imagine, she is furious with your mother. I am, too, but I long ago made peace with that, which is why I was focused more on finding you than finding who took you. But Elaine . . ."

I didn't reply as I just stared at him.

"Anyway," he managed a smile. "One thing that I want to make clear is that your struggle days are over."

"So, even if I don't sign the contract, that offer still stands?"

He looked like he didn't know how to answer that. Finally, he said, "I recognize that it was difficult to put Virginia in a home, and I know letting her go won't be easy, but you are about to embark on a whole new life.'

I didn't know if he just assumed I was cutting my mother off, or trying to convince himself. As far as I was concerned, putting my mother in a home was a compromise. But no way was I signing a contract banning all future contact with her.

"Nothing would make me happier," he continued, "than to be able to give you, Malcolm, and Destiny the life that you deserve."

Then, his eyes lit up like he had an idea. "As a matter of fact, why don't you come stay in the guest house? Malcolm told me about the problems with your apartment. A drive-by shooting? You can't stay there. Think about Destiny. You have money now. Your husband has a good job now. You can go find your own place. You can have something built. But for now, until that happens, you're more than welcome to stay in the guest house. In fact, we insist. If Malcom is going to be working here, it makes sense rather than an hour and a half commute."

I nodded again. I wasn't really sure how to reply. I didn't really want to live with them. But it would solve an array of problems.

"Okay. I'll talk with Malcolm and see what he says," I said.

My father's grin was instant.

Chapter 30

I heard the door slam so hard it rattled the pictures on the wall in the kitchen.

"What's going on, babe?" I said, drying my eyes as I walked out of the kitchen. My husband was fuming as he paced back and forth.

"You know the guy across the hall? The one I call Ike Turner?"

I nodded.

"Yeah, he just ran into my car as he was backing out. With his big old Ford F150. Then, he had the nerve to get out and flex on me like I was the one in the wrong." Malcolm paced back and forth across the room.

"What?" I said. "How bad is the damage?"

He ran his hands over his smooth head like he was trying to calm himself down. "It's still drivable, but he knocked my bumper off, dented my door and get this . . ." He turned and looked me directly in the eye. "I asked for his insurance and this dude pulled a gun on me."

"What?" I screamed, then lowered my voice before I woke up Destiny. "Are you kidding me?"

I couldn't believe this. First a drive-by, then this?

"I swear to God I can't stand this place," he mumbled.

I bit my bottom lip.

He turned to me. "Babe, you know I don't want to pressure you, but you might need to hurry up and make a decision. We need to cash that check so that we can hurry up and get out of here."

I took a deep breath. I had been putting off talking to him about going to stay at Major and Elaine's guest house. He'd had such a good first day at work. I didn't want to present an option that I hadn't deemed completely feasible just yet. But this could've ended tragically today.

"Yeah, about that," I began, deciding enough was enough. "Major actually suggested that we move in with them."

"Are you serious?"

"Not in their home, per se. But he said we could live in the guest house. It's bigger than this apartment, so . . ."

"So . . . when are we leaving?" he exclaimed.

I should've known that would be his reaction. "Are you sure that's wise, though?"

"Babe," he stepped toward me, "our daughter could've been killed in a drive-by shooting. I could've been killed just trying to come home. So either we need to cash that check and let the chips fall where they may, or we need to take your father up on his offer."

"You'll get a paycheck soon."

"They get paid at the beginning of the month. That's three weeks from now. Do you know all that could happen in those three weeks? And I don't want to ask anyone for an advance."

I knew he was right. I took a deep breath. "Fine. We can move."

My husband pumped his fist in delight. "You don't understand the peace of mind that's going to give us, and we don't even have to stress about the rent this month."

I simply nodded. "I'm fixing dinner because your sister is coming by." I hadn't seen Kendra in a few weeks, so I welcomed her visit.

Malcolm kissed me on the cheek, and judging from his excitement, he raced upstairs to pack.

Twenty minutes later, I heard a knock on the door. I raced over to open it. My mother-in-law stood next to Kendra.

"Hello, Jill. I decided to tag along," she said, before pushing her way inside. "My son!" She extended her arms to Malcolm, who was coming down the stairs. "How are you, baby?"

I looked at Kendra and she mouthed "Sorry," then held up a bag. "But I brought wine, though. Stella Rosa Black."

"Thanks, we're going to need it," I whispered.

I could tell my sister-in-law had baby fever the way she was bouncing Destiny on her lap. She noticed me staring at her and said, "Yes, my ovaries are in overdrive."

Mrs. Reed laughed. "I told her that she needs to go ahead and give me some more grandbabies." She glanced over my shoulder, noticing the small holes in the living room wall. "Jesus, are those from the drive-by shooting?"

I nodded.

"Oh, my. You all need to move asap," Mrs. Reed said.

Malcolm appeared by my side. We exchanged glances and I gave him a nod to share the news.

"Speaking of that, we have some news to tell you guys," Malcolm said, putting his arm around me.

"Oh my God, you're pregnant?" Mrs. Reed said with excitement.

"No, it's not that," Malcolm laughed.

She slumped back in her chair, pouting. Mrs. Reed would be happy if each of her children gave her five or six grandchildren, even though she wasn't exactly the type of grandma that would keep kids all summer. She was the come by, kiss them, and keep it moving type.

"We've been going through some things," Malcolm continued, causing both Kendra and his mother's expressions to turn serious.

"What's wrong?" Kendra said.

"You're not sick, are you?" Mrs. Reed said, panic immediately setting in.

"No, Mom, would you let me finish?" he replied. They both fell silent and he continued. "Jill and I recently had some discoveries about her family." He squeezed my hand as he spoke. "Several years ago there was this kidnapping in Beaumont, a biracial baby from a wealthy family. It was a pretty big story in the area. Well, we recently discovered that Jill is that kidnapped child."

"What?" both Kendra and her mother exclaimed.

"So Mama Connie isn't your mother?" Kendra asked.

I shook my head.

"She stole you from those people," Mrs. Reed said. "No way."

My eyes teared up. Mrs. Reed's eyes met her son's and their unspoken communication caused her to fall quiet as she took my hand and patted it. "Oh, sweetie, I'm so sorry."

Kendra handed Destiny to her mother and walked over to hug me. I choked back my words and nodded because if I opened my mouth, I'd start crying.

Malcolm continued, "Well, naturally this discovery has led to a lot of changes in our lives. Jill's biological family is extremely rich and they want her to share in the fortune. I have taken a job with Logan Industries, the family business. It's a good job."

Mrs. Reed fanned herself. "Wow, so you mean to tell me that you guys are now rich?"

"Kinda sorta," Malcolm said. "Jill's family is anyway, but this job is good and well, our lives will be changing a bit. We will be moving to Beaumont."

"Beaumont?"

"It's just an hour and a half away," he said. "That's where I'll be working and we'll end up getting our own place. But in the meantime, we'll be staying in the Logans' guest house."

I could tell Kendra and Mrs. Reed were dumbfounded. I got it. It would take me a moment to come to terms with the new course of my life, too.

Chapter 31

Maybe it was all the crime shows I watched, but I was convinced someone knew about the money my father had given me and was scoping me out. Maybe they planned to kidnap Destiny and demand ransom. Whatever it was, I couldn't shake the feeling that I was being followed. I'd first felt like someone was following me in the grocery store after I'd returned from lunch with my father yesterday. I'd blown it off as an overactive imagination. But when I'd spotted the woman with long burgundy-tinted hair, butterscotch-colored skin, and a body that screamed daily cardio workouts, my antenna went up. This was definitely the same woman from the grocery store. And now, looking at her trying to be inconspicuous as she followed me through the mall, I also remembered her coming into Starbucks recently.

I'd been talking to Cynthia on my cell when I spotted her several feet behind me.

"Okay. I know that I'm not crazy," I whispered into my microphone. "That same woman I told you I thought was following me the other day in the grocery store is here at the mall. I thought I was being paranoid behind learning I'd been kidnapped. But this woman is for real following me. Do you think she's trying to kidnap Destiny?" I asked in horror.

"No, I do not," Cynthia replied. "But I do know I'm the paranoid one. So if you think someone is following you, someone is following you. If I were you, I would go confront her and ask her what she wants."

"But what if she tells me I'm crazy and she doesn't know what I'm talking about," I whispered.

Cynthia tsked. "What if she does? You don't know that woman. You'll never see her again so you have nothing to lose."

"And what if she says she is following me?"

"Then you bust her in her eye." From the tone of my best friend's voice, I could tell she was serious.

I don't know why I found that so funny. Maybe because I'd been so on edge lately. Malcolm was sinking further and further into the Logans' web. They'd given him a company car, a Cadillac STS. And since it was ten times better than the 2003 Honda Accord he'd been driving since we met, my husband was on cloud nine. And I now knew all hopes of getting my husband to think objectively were out the window. Thank goodness Major had given him a sign-on bonus. It was only ten thousand, but since it was more money than we had ever seen at one time, it was a lifesaver and it was enough to keep Malcolm from harassing me about cashing that check.

"Okay. What mall are you at? The Galleria? You know, since you're rich and all." Cynthia laughed.

"No, I'm not at the Galleria and I'm not rich. My biological parents are," I replied.

"Whatever. That means you're rich. As long as you're not at Sharpstown Mall, you're fine. Then I would really worry about you being followed."

"Is that even a mall anymore?" I said. "But no. I'm at First Colony."

"Okay. Cool. Why don't you go into one of those kiddie stores, like The Children's Place? That way if she follows you in, then you know she's following you."

"What if she says she has kids, too?"

"Then you know she's lying. And so you're justified to bust her in the eye."

I ignored my friend's violent solution and said, "Okay. Gymboree is right here," I said, glancing back at the woman who had suddenly stopped and was looking at stuff at a kiosk.

"Keep me on the phone," Cynthia said.

I did as my friend instructed and eased into the Gymboree store and started looking at the little girl's clothes.

"Oh my God," I whispered. "She came in here."

"Unh unh. For real, you need to go confront her."

"What am I supposed to say?" I asked as the woman casually walked into the store. It was so obvious now that she was following me.

"Just walk up to her and say, 'What's up?' If it's nothing, she will say, 'Excuse me, I don't know what you're talking about.' If it's something, you punch her in her eye." I could picture my best friend feverishly pacing across her apartment. "Just walk up to her and repeat after me."

"Cynthia . . ."

"Girl, do it. Tell her that you know she's been following you," Cynthia said. I had no idea why she was whispering. "Tell her if she doesn't back of off you, you will put those Taekwondo skills to use."

"I never took Taekwondo."

"She doesn't know that. Just do it."

I summoned my inner Cynthia and approached the woman. I was ready for her denial and my subsequent embarrassment. "Excuse me," I said. "Do I know you?"

She crossed her arms and glared at me. "Do you?" she replied.

"Is she getting smart with you?" Cynthia asked.

I wanted to tell Cynthia that I got it from here but I didn't want the woman to know someone was in my ear.

"It seems like you've been following me," I told the woman, stepping closer to her.

She rolled her eyes. "And it seems you're invading my personal space," the woman had the nerve to say to me.

Now was my turn to say, "Excuse me?"

"I'm just in here shopping for kids' clothes and you're in my personal space." She motioned around her like she had a legitimate claim to the space around her.

My left eyebrow went up. "Well, since I've seen you a number of occasions, I'm really feeling like you're stalking me," I said. "So, naturally, I'm trying to figure out why."

"That's what I'm talking about," Cynthia said in my ear. "Tell her you're no fool."

"Please, don't flatter yourself," the woman said. She swung her long hair over her shoulder. Either she had some amazing genes to give her tresses like that, or she had paid top dollar for a weave. "But I don't need to stalk anyone, especially the likes of you."

"Oh, hell no!" Cynthia exclaimed. "Did she just say what I thought she said? What mall are you at again? I'm on my way!"

I ignored my friend as I said, "Look, what is your problem, lady? It's obvious that you're following me and I'd like to know why?"

She folded her arms, rolled her eyes again, and said, "What are you to Major?"

I frowned in confusion. "Excuse me?"

"You heard me. I didn't stutter," the woman said.

It was my turn to fold my arms and glare at her. "So that's what this is about. Wow. What I am to Major is none of your business."

The woman jabbed a finger in my direction. "The wife I can deal with, but he is not going to be cheating on me with the likes of you."

I almost burst out laughing but didn't want to give her that satisfaction. "Lady, I don't know who you are and why you are following me but you're so far off base it's not even funny."

It was her turn to take a step into my personal space. "Let me tell you what's off base. I have played my position with Major for years. And I'll be damned if I let some little"—she looked me up and down— "thot come along and take what's rightfully mine."

"Hit her in the eye," Cynthia screamed.

"Seems like since you're the other woman," I replied, continuing to ignore my friend, "nothing would be rightfully yours."

She stepped so close to me, our noses could've done the Tango. "Don't play with me, little girl."

The woman couldn't have been any more than ten years older than me, so the little girl comment was baffling.

"If you don't back up off me . . ." I said.

"Back up?" Cynthia shouted. "Oh, hell no!"

I know my friend was about to blow a gasket, but I couldn't focus on her.

"How long have you been messing around with Major?" the woman demanded to know. Her eyes scanned me in disdain. "Why he would want to be messing with a Starbucks barista is beyond me."

Wow, so this woman really had been stalking me.

"Answer me!" she demanded.

I inhaled, reminded myself that I was in the middle of a children's store, and said. "You know what? These are questions you need to ask Major yourself."

"You know what?" she said, mocking me as she pulled out her cell phone, "I will ask Major myself. I'll get him on the phone right now."

In my ear Cynthia was shouting so loud that I was sure the woman heard her. "Are you freaking kidding me? Is this really happening? FaceTime me so I can see."

If I hadn't been so pissed, I would've cracked up at Cynthia's reaction. I was glad that my best friend wasn't here because this would so escalate out of control. Though my friend was the college educated professional one, she was most likely to administer a beatdown.

"Yeah, I'm going to let him know I know about you and there

won't be any way of finagling out of this. Because trust me, if it comes down to Major choosing me or you, he's going to choose me."

Her confidence made me find my funny bone. "Sweetheart, I promise you he won't." I laughed.

That seemed to enrage her even more. "Oh, we're about to see about that."

I thought the woman was dialing Major's cell, but I was stunned when his face popped up on the screen and I heard him say, "Hey, what's going on?"

The woman's demeanor instantly changed and she flashed a seductive smile. "Hey baby," she said. "How is your day going?"

"It is fine. How can I help you?" The formality of his voice caused her lips to turn downward.

"Why are you talking to me like that?" she whined.

"I'm in the middle of something. What's going on, Stephanie?"

"I'm in the middle of something, too," she said, her attitude resurfacing. "I'm here with your little thot and I'm letting her know, and you know, that this thing the two of you have going on isn't happening."

"What little thot? What in the world are you talking about?" Major said. I could hear the exasperation in his voice.

"This thot," she said, turning the camera toward me.

I cocked my head, waved and said, "Hi, Daddy." It was my first time calling him daddy, but it couldn't have been more fitting.

"And is she calling you daddy?" the woman said, turning the phone back around to her, her anger meter on ten now. "Oh, hell no. Are you for real?"

By this time Cynthia was dying laughing. "Oh my God. Did she Facetime him? I knew I loved those air pods I gave you for your birthday. I hear everything. I wish this was being recorded. You could so go viral."

"Yes, I call him daddy," I told the woman, ignoring my friend as I leaned into the camera's view. I guess he was too shocked to realize that I'd called him daddy for the first time. "Daddy, your mistress is stalking and harassing me at the mall."

I could tell she was about to go in rare form when my father bellowed, "Have you lost your damn mind? I told you this craziness is unacceptable and I don't do this ghetto mess."

"Well, I told you. I've been waiting a long time and I'm not going—"

"And this is not the way to handle this," he said, cutting her off. "I do not believe this." His chastisement actually brought her level down a notch.

"But you're out here seeing other women," she pouted. "You promised that there was no one else."

Major took a deep breath, pursed his lips, then said, "Stephanie, she called me daddy because that's my daughter. My. Daughter. And as I told you before, this isn't working so please do not call me again or I promise I will have you arrested." He hung the phone up.

She stood there with a confused look on her face. "His d-daughter?"

I couldn't help but smile. "Yes." I shrugged. "So now let's see who he chooses, me or his psychopath mistress. You have a nice day," I said, as I turned and walked out of the store while my best friend shouted cheers in my ear.

Chapter 32

Now that the reality TV moment had worn off, reality hit me like a mack truck. My father had a mistress. And I was packing my belongings to move in with my angry mother and cheating father. What in the world was I getting myself into?

I was asleep when Malcolm got home last night so I hadn't been able to fill him in until this morning.

"I guess you just never know with some people," Malcolm said.

I could tell already that as far as my husband was concerned, Major Logan could have all the women he wanted and Malcolm wouldn't utter a bad word about him. Malcolm loved his job and he'd had a pitch meeting with the Logan Investments Executive Board that he felt had gone well. So I could probably tell Malcolm that Major shot Barack Obama and he wouldn't care.

"So, I'm assuming it's just who he is—a cheater," I said. "First my mother, now Elaine."

"You never know what's going on in someone's relationship," was my husband's response.

I side-eyed his attempt to absolve my father. "I actually feel bad for Elaine. No one deserves that. I don't understand. Why don't men just leave rather than cheat?" I said.

Malcolm pulled me toward him. "How about we stay out of

their marriage and we focus on ours." He flashed that cheesy grin that had captured my heart from day one. It's a new start, baby. We don't have to worry about a stray bullet coming through and hurting one of us, or worse, hitting Destiny. We're finally about to get the life we deserve. Let's embrace it."

I sighed. "Yeah, but why don't we just get our own place? I just felt some kind of way about moving in with them."

The neighbors had been arguing again last night and we'd barely been able to sleep in fear that something would jump off, so I knew we had to go. I just still wasn't sure going to the home of parents I barely knew was the answer. I wanted to get to know them. But I felt like they were rushing me. Plus, the more time I was around them, the sooner I was going to have to bring up my mother and I didn't want to lie to them.

To his credit, Major had offered to buy us a house outright. But that had been one thing that Malcolm had been adamant about. He wanted to work so that he could contribute to a house of our own. He told Major that he wouldn't feel right until he had something to bring to the table. Of course, my father loved that.

"It's just temporary, baby. You're the one who doesn't want to cash this check yet." He pursed his lips like all I needed to do was say the word and we'd detour to the bank on our way to our new home.

"You know that I'm hesitant because of their stipulations. I don't want anyone making me completely cut off contact with my mother. I know you have so many things you'd like to do with that money but until they agree with the contract, we just have to pretend that check doesn't exist."

He kept his smile. "Yes, that money is awesome, but with the sign-on bonus and the fact that I'm working a good job, we'll be okay for the time being. That check can take us to the next level. But this money will help us get on our feet. It will give you time to decide what you want to do about the check."

"Thank you for understanding," I said, standing on my toes so that our lips could meet. Our quick kiss turned into a long, passionate one, that made me pull back and say, "Whoa, okay. Let's dial it back or we'll never finish getting this stuff packed. We'll end up on that bare mattress."

He popped me on the behind. "And would that be a bad thing?"

I giggled as I placed some glasses in a box.

"Real talk, babe, I know this is hard for you," Malcolm said, grabbing the tape and closing one of the boxes. "And I know you don't want to turn your back on your mother and by no means am I suggesting that you should. You know how much I want this money, but I don't want that to play a role in your decision. Do what you feel is right."

Before I could thank my husband for being so amazing, Malcolm's cell phone rang. His eyes grew wide as he turned the phone toward me. "Logan Investment Group" popped up on the screen.

"Oh, my goodness. Put them on speaker."

Malcolm pressed the speaker button. "This is Malcolm Reed."

I smiled at how official my man sounded. "Malcolm, this is Wallace Waterberry."

"What kind of name is Waterberry?" I mouthed.

Malcolm shushed me and said, "Yes, sir, good afternoon. It's a pleasure to hear from you."

"Pardon my reaching out to you on a Saturday, but our board meeting just wrapped up and we reviewed your proposal. I must say, your presentation on Wednesday was impressive and after discussing it, the board would like to talk to you further about investing in your app development."

My husband released a silent scream, matched by my silent cheer.

"Thank you, sir," Malcolm said.

"Your proposal has been forwarded to our development team. We'd like you to meet with our developers on Monday morning.

They will compile a team to properly execute your plan," Mr. Waterberry said.

"Mr. Reed, we're not just saying this because of your relationship to our chairman. That got you the in the door, but this decision is purely on your own merits. We feel like this app will be the next big thing. Congratulations."

"Thank you, sir," Malcolm repeated. I think I saw tears well in my husband's eyes.

Mr. Waterberry continued, "We'll talk with Major on Monday but we might need to do some readjustment with that maintenance job because we will need you to focus all your time and efforts on this development project; of course you will be paid a generous wage, in addition to the high six-figure fee we will pay for acquiring the app, and the ongoing percentage you will receive based on the app's success. But of course, our attorneys can work all of that out."

"Yes, sir," my husband said. His hands were actually shaking as he held the phone. "Yes, sir."

"So, we'll see you on Monday."

"Yes, sir. See you then."

Malcolm disconnected the call and released the screams he'd been holding in.

"Yesssss!!!" he shouted as he picked me up and swung me around. His happiness was contagious and I squealed with him. "How long have I been sitting on this idea?"

"Forever," I replied.

He set me down, kissed me again, and started pacing through the kitchen.

"So many people could get ahead in life if only they had a chance. Just like Major got a chance, a helping hand, and it turned his life around. That's what's about to happen. A chance, that's what so many brothers like me need."

"Well, you got it, babe. And I have no doubt that you will

make the best of it," I told him, hugging him. I felt years of stress escape from his body.

"I don't know how long it will take them to process everything, but just be patient," he said. "We won't even fully unpack at the Logans' estate because I will move you into the Reed estate as soon as possible."

I threw my hands around my husband's neck and showed my gratitude with kisses. That was music to my ears.

Chapter 33

I couldn't believe that I was living in a mansion. Well, I wasn't technically *in* the mansion. I was in the guest house in the back of the mansion. But this guest house was bigger than any place I'd ever lived in before and Malcolm was loving every minute of it. I had reminded him that this was only temporary because we were moving into the "Reed Estate" as soon as possible.

Both Major and Elaine had been giddy with excitement when the small U-Haul backed up to the guest house. Phillip watched with his nose turned up as the movers unloaded our meager belongings. It was almost as if he was horrified that we would bring our tattered furniture anywhere near this palatial estate.

I thought about my father as I continued unpacking boxes. He'd apologized profusely about Stephanie and I could tell he was embarrassed. He tried to explain his way around it, saying the situation was "complicated." I saved him the effort of trying to lie and told him that it wasn't my business and his secret was safe. The whole situation made me uncomfortable, but Malcolm convinced me to leave it alone for now.

I wondered if I would've been able to do that if he had cheated on my mother, Connie. Was I able to keep such a secret because I still didn't feel a connection to Elaine? Would I ever feel a connection to Elaine?

My unanswered thoughts were interrupted by Destiny's whimpering. I went over to her swing and picked her up. "What's the matter, pumpkin? You don't like our new house?" I cooed. She'd been fussy since we arrived two days ago. I was convinced that she didn't want to be here either. Malcolm swore it was me manifesting my own displeasure about the move but I didn't think so.

The doorbell rang and I pulled my daughter close as I went to answer it. I didn't recognize the petite blonde woman waving to me as I peeked through the screen.

"Hello," I said, opening the door. In order to get to the guest house, you had to be let into the gated estate, then take the walkway up to the guest house, so I figured whoever this woman was, she couldn't be too bad.

"Hello, I'm Marguerite," the woman said in a thick Swedish accent.

I shifted Destiny to my other hip. "Hi, Marguerite. How can I help you?"

"The Mrs. sent me here to help you with young Destiny."

"I'm sorry?" I said, confused.

"I am your nanny." She leaned over to look behind me like she was surveying my house. "May I come in?"

"Nanny?" I said, not moving. I was a little taken aback. No one had talked to me about a nanny. "I'm sorry. There must be some sort of misunderstanding," I told her. "I didn't hire a nanny."

"No, no misunderstanding," she replied. "I'm supposed to start today. Mrs. Logan insisted that I be here by noon to feed young Miss Destiny." She glanced at her watch. "I know it's just eleven forty-five, but I believe to be early is to be on time and to be on time is to be late."

I wasn't interested in this woman's motivational quotes. I was trying to figure out why Elaine thought it would be okay to hire a nanny without first talking to me.

She started digging in her bag. "If you're concerned, just know that I have my Master's in childcare and development. I am certified in CPR and first aid, and have twelve certificates of trainings," she said, handing me her resume. "I was young Phillip's nanny."

I took her resume, still shaking my head. "Okay, that's nice. But I still didn't hire you. Where is Mrs. Logan?"

"She's in the main house."

Destiny started crying. "Shh. Be quiet, sweetie. I need to talk to the lady," I said, jiggling her on my hip as I glanced at the woman's extensive resume.

"Here, may I?" Marguerite extended her hands for Destiny. I hesitated as images of my mother, clad in a disguise, plotting to abduct me, flashed through my mind.

Marguerite smiled. "I understand your hesitation." She reached in her bag and pulled out another folder, which she opened to reveal several photos.

"This is Master Phillip as a child." She pointed to a picture of her standing next to a little boy in a sailor's outfit. Even then, he wore a scowl. Marguerite pulled another picture to the front. It was the younger version of Marguerite again, this time, holding a baby in a white gown. The baby's eyes were wide and she wore a big, dimpled smile. "And that . . . that is you," she said. "A week before you went missing."

I took the photo and had to steady myself. My mother had baby pictures of me, but they all started around when I was one year old. This . . . this hammered home how I had once belonged to someone else. Then, the barrage of "what ifs" hit me. What if I had grown up in this life? What if Marguerite had been my nanny? What if I'd grown up a Logan?

Destiny squirmed and started full-on crying, pulling me out of my trance. Marguerite stepped near me. "May I?" she repeated.

I think I was still in shock because I simply nodded and handed my daughter to her as I continued staring at the picture.

Marguerite started singing some song in a foreign language and her voice instantly soothed Destiny.

I shook off the "what if" dance and returned my attention to the issue at hand. "I need to go talk to Mrs. Logan."

"Well, I can sit here with Destiny while you do that," she replied.

I raised an eyebrow, which caused her to smile and say, "My car is parked out front. I would have to come through the house to go anywhere. I couldn't leave with her. Trust me, I've been with the Logan family for thirty years." She paused, then solemnly added, "I was your nanny before you went missing. I want only the best for you."

I swallowed the lump in my throat and said, "Okay, I'll be right back."

I dashed toward the main house, prepared to give Elaine a piece of my mind and let her know that she couldn't make decisions about my daughter without me. I had just reached the back door and was about to tap when I saw her and Phillip in the kitchen.

"You are the dumbest human being I know," Elaine yelled, causing my hand to drop from mid-air when I was about to knock. "I don't understand how somebody so ignorant can have a college degree. That's why you're single and living off of us. No woman wants your useless behind."

Phillip's voice was calm as he said, "Auntie, put the drink down."

"You don't tell me what to do. I tell you what to do." I was shocked because it sounded like her words were slurred. For the first time since I'd met her, she didn't seem poised and put together.

"I thought that you had stopped drinking," he said.

"Do I pay you to think?" she snapped. "No, I don't."

"I'm family." He wasn't showing it, but I could tell her words pierced him.

She laughed. "And you wouldn't be here if it wasn't for the money. Don't think I don't know that. The only reason you hang around is because you want my money."

"You think everybody wants your money," Phillip said, reaching for her glass. She moved it out of his reach and swatted his hand.

"Just leave me alone," she barked. "I don't want you here. Nobody wants you, that's why the family pawned you off on us like some kind of consolation prize for losing my daughter."

Phillip released a frustrated sigh, but his reaction showed he was used to this treatment. "Aunt Elaine, I promised Uncle Major that I would look after you. And you promised us that you would stop drinking."

"I am not a damn child," she said. "I don't need anybody to watch after me."

"I thought that since you got your precious daughter back that you would stay sober."

She laughed, a maniacal, hollow laugh. "My precious daughter? Oh, you mean the one who doesn't even want to acknowledge me."

"I can't blame her," Phillip mumbled.

Before I could blink, Elaine reached out and slapped him across the face. I jumped, knocking over a plant by the back door in the process. That caused both of them to turn their attention to the door. I didn't know what to do. I stood frozen until Elaine set down her glass and said, "Alicia, what are you doing?" She opened the back door and gave me a hug. The smell of liquor permeated her body.

"I-I just came to ask you about the n-nanny," I stammered.

"Oh, you saw Marguerite?" she said. "Perfect. She's going to be great for Destiny."

"But I didn't ask for a nanny," I said, flashing an uneasy look at Phillip.

"But you need one." She patted my cheek. "You're a Logan, sweetheart. We have people to help with all of our trivial work."

"Taking care of my daughter is not trivial work," I replied.

"Nonsense." She wobbled, steadied herself, then added, "You're just not accustomed to life's luxuries."

"No, I don't need her," I said. "I'm at home with Destiny and when I go to work, I can take her to daycare."

"Work?" Elaine balked like I had said something blasphemous. "Surely you're not planning to go back to that god-awful job."

I stared at her in shock. "That god-awful job paid my bills," I finally said.

"Sweetheart, you don't need to worry about bills anymore." She laughed. "Your life of poverty and struggle is over. You are now living the life you should've always lived. The one you would have had, had that dreadful woman not stolen you."

I gritted my teeth. It was obvious that she was intoxicated but liquor released true feelings. "I may have been poor but I didn't live a life of poverty," I replied.

"Same thing, to-mato, tom-ahto," she said, waving my words off.

This wasn't the same woman who just a few days ago had been gentle and ecstatic to welcome me back into her life. I glanced at the half-empty glass and wondered if this was the real Elaine. Is this why my father was out cheating? Or is this how she coped with his cheating?

"Well, I just came by to tell you that I didn't need the nanny and so—"

"Nonsense," she repeated, cutting me off. "She's here, and she's here to stay. Would you like something to drink?"

I saw Phillip roll his eyes. I debated speaking to him but I wasn't in the mood to fake the funk. So I just said, "No, I'm good."

"Well, I'll just have to drink yours," she giggled as she refilled her glass with a clear liquid. "Remember dinner is promptly at six."

That caused me to frown again. "I don't usually eat that early."

"Well, that's how we do things around here. So, we'll see you at six," she said, taking her glass and heading toward the kitchen entrance. "I'm going to lie down. I have a bear of a headache."

I stood there in the kitchen trying to understand what had just happened. It was almost as if a completely different woman had taken over Elaine's body. I looked at Phillip. He shook his head and said, "Welcome to the Logan family." And then turned and walked out of the room.

Chapter 34

Seeing the real Elaine had made me miss the woman who would always be my "real" mother. But I had to get the rest of the blanks filled in. I had to truly understand my mother's mindset so that I could begin to forgive her, so that I could heal from her betrayal.

That's why I was now standing in front of my mother's new home. The beautiful estate was like a utopia. From the freshly manicured grass to the butterflies that looked like they had been implanted into the scenery. This place was magnificent. It was better than anything I could have ever given my mother on my own. So, for that I was grateful, especially because more than anything, The Westerly Estates was better than a twelve-by-twelve cell.

I took a deep breath and made my way up the walkway. This was my first visit here. The counselor had suggested that I wait two weeks to come see my mother to give her time to get acclimated. I know she thought that I had abandoned her. But truthfully, I needed this time myself to come to terms with what she had done.

"Hi," I said to the smiling lady at the front desk. I'm Jillian Reed. I'm here to see my mother, Connie Harrison." The minute I said her name, a voice in my head reminded me that wasn't her real name.

"Oh yes, Ms. Connie," the perky woman said. "She's not too happy. But most of our patients aren't when they first arrive here. Maybe your presence will cheer her up. We haven't gotten her to do much since she's been here."

I nodded because if I opened my mouth, I would cry. The thought of my mother being in this place, sad and feeling abandoned, tore at my insides. She might not have had the class and money of Elaine Logan but she had a joy that was unmatched.

Had.

Because I'd abandoned her and stolen her joy.

"You're more than welcome to go back to her room," the nurse said. "The last door down the hall to the right."

"Thank you," I managed to mutter. I walked to the edge of the hall in trepidation. My mother's door was cracked. I tapped on it. There was no reply, so I eased the door open and looked inside. My mother sat with her back toward the door looking out onto the beautiful lawn. She rocked back and forth in a wicker rocking chair. I expected her to turn when she heard her door open, but she just continued rocking.

"Mama?" I said.

She stopped rocking but she didn't turn to look my way.

"Mama?" I repeated as I stepped into the room. "It's me, Jill."

She paused, and then she continued rocking. I swallowed the lump in my throat and eased toward the side of her.

"How are you doing?" I said, taking her hand.

She gently eased her hand away from me.

"Everything going okay?" I pulled up a chair and took a seat next to her.

She just continued rocking.

"So now you're mad at me and not going to talk?" I asked. "Okay, I understand," I added after she still didn't respond. "You're mad. As much as this hurts, it's for the best." I paused as I looked around the room. "This place is nice. You have to admit that."

Finally, she turned to me and said, "Your place was nicer."

"It was not, Mother," I told her. "You said yourself that it was a bad area. And we're no longer there anyway."

"What?" she said, finally turning her attention to me.

"We moved. You know it was a struggle for us. And with everything going on . . . well, we'd been trying to figure out what we were going to do."

"Moved where?" she said. My silence was her answer. "In with them, Major and Elaine?" she spit their name like venom. If I didn't know better, I would think they were the ones that had stolen me from her. I decided now wasn't the time to get into my housing situation with my mother because there was no way that conversation would end well.

"So, Mama. How have things been going?" I asked.

"They're going. But don't act like you care," she snapped. "You haven't even been here."

"I couldn't come for the first two weeks. Remember the counselor told us that?"

"It doesn't matter. You tossed me aside so it doesn't really matter." She resumed rocking.

"Please don't be like this," I said. "You have to understand the position you placed me in. It was either this or jail."

She tensed up at the word jail.

"The Logans are furious with you, especially Elaine. She wants you to spend the rest of your life in prison." My mother's hands started shaking a bit as she rocked back and forth. "And I checked, Mama. If she really pushed for it, you could spend up to thirty years in prison."

"I did what I felt was right," she said. But her voice no longer had the confidence that it had the last time she told me that.

"But it was wrong," I said.

She continued rocking.

"Mama, I need to understand why. I mean, the journal gave me some insight, but I need to hear from you. How you could just lie to me my whole life." I waited for her to say something. When she didn't, I continued, "Can you please talk to me?"

She turned and poked her lips out as she looked out the window again.

"You owe me that much," I said. "You stole my life from me, Mama."

"I gave you a life," she said, shifting her head back around to face me. Her eyes misted up as she said, "I knew you were destined for a horrible life with them."

"How in the world can you say that? The kind of life they could have given me is the stuff people dream of." Even as the words left my mouth, I thought about Elaine's drunken fight with Phillip.

"What kind of life is that?" my mother snapped. "One that their money bought?" She let out a convoluted laugh. "Money is not the key to happiness." She took a deep breath like she was trying to calm herself down. "I know what I did was wrong. But I will always believe in my heart it was the right thing to do." She stopped rocking again and for a moment, I thought she was going to completely shut down. But she simply said, "You're right. I do owe you an explanation. And before the good Lord snatches what is left of my mind, I want to give you one." She stood and turned her rocking chair to face me.

She continued, "You read my journal. You know why I did what I did, but what you don't understand is that I truly believed that you were going to be better off with me than them. I never set out to take you when I first started following her. Yes, I was distraught over Major. At one point I knew I was spiraling out of control, that's when I checked myself into the mental hospital. I thought I made progress, but I made the mistake of driving to Beaumont on a visit home. I don't know why. I just did." She stood and walked over to the sink in her room, grabbed a paper towel, wet it and dabbed her face. "When I saw him with her, my heart was crushed into a million pieces all over again," she continued. "I became obsessed with her. I wanted to know what it was about her. I blamed it on her being white, rich, everything. I knew her family was wealthy, but she was no prettier than me. She was no smarter than me. And she couldn't have possibly loved Major more than I did. So I was desperate to understand what it was about her. I followed her everywhere. I actually moved to Beaumont and stayed there for six months. I watched her as her belly swelled. I watched her as she gave birth. And then I watched her, not even two months after you came into the world, take you to the park. You were too young to be out with all those germy kids. But she didn't care. She just had to go meet her friends and her sister. And you sat there and nobody paid you any attention. And when you cried, they were too busy taking pictures to care."

I wanted to interrupt her but I was afraid she would lose her train of thought.

"I watched and I waited," she continued, then turned to face me. "I fought the urge to tell her, 'Don't you know you should pick her up and comfort her,' and then her sister laughed and said, 'I always heard little mulatto babies were harder to raise,' and I was floored. I expected Elaine to say something. To go off, to chastise her sister, and she just sat there. One of her friends was the only one to say, 'that was mean.' And her sister said 'she needs to get used to it because once Mother Madeline sees the child, she will be hearing a lot worse.'"

My mother inhaled, exhaled, then continued, "I knew then that you would be subjected to a lifetime of racism. And based on Elaine's reaction, she wouldn't protect you. No child should be subjected to that. So I stepped in. I had prayed for God to give me a sign on how to break free from Major, and that day in the park, as I sat on that bench and I watched and listened, they didn't even care that there was a black woman within hearing distance when they made the comment. They continued with their vile and racist comments. Like it was a joke. And I decided that day, that I would save you."

I was quiet. There was nothing in Elaine's demeanor, her actions that said she was racist. She wouldn't have been married to a black man this long if she were racist. My mother must have been reading my mind because she said, "In the end we will remember not the words of our enemies but the silence of our friends. That's a quote from Martin Luther King, Jr. Maybe Elaine was the black sheep of the family. Pun intended. But she was silent as her family berated her only child. I didn't want you raised in that environment. With a mother that failed to protect you. A mother more concerned with hanging out with her friends. You were a prop and she didn't deserve you."

I could tell from the determined look on my mother's face she meant every word she said.

I had come to my mother for answers. And she'd given them to me. The question now was—what was I supposed to do with that information?

Chapter 35

This was something I had dreamed of my whole life. A room full of my family members. Aunts and uncles, cousins, and the like. Elaine had summoned every relative within a hundred-mile radius for a "coming home" party. At first, I was all for it, but right now, in this sea of strangers, and knowing what my mother had told me a few days ago, I was questioning why I'd agreed to this.

I shook off the fact that this didn't feel like family and chalked it up to the fact that I was a new implant. Malcolm seemed to be blending right in. Right now, he was talking sports with one of my second cousins outside on the veranda.

I sat bouncing Destiny on my lap. Elaine had positioned me in a seat that looked like a throne, right at the front of the living room so that each family member could come greet me as they entered. It felt pretentious to me, but she insisted. Still, the whole thing was making me uncomfortable.

A flutter of nervousness swept through me as Elaine's grandmother made her way toward me. She'd been the last to arrive to this family gathering that had Elaine running around, barking orders at staff all evening. At first, I thought the chaotic quest for perfection was for me, but Elaine had said several times that everything had to be "just right for Mother Madeline."

Mother Madeline had to be in her nineties, but still stood like she had descended from royalty. And the way everyone catered to her, I had no doubt she was the nucleus of the family's wealth.

"Well, I'll be," she said as she approached me. Her expression was neutral. No, stoic was a better word. She wore a beaded black dress and a gray fur stole and pearls that probably cost more than I'd made in the last three years. "I never thought this day would come."

I expected her to embrace me like everyone else had. But instead, she simply said, "Stand up, let me take a look at you."

I did as I was told, intimidated just like the rest of the family.

"Turn around," she demanded.

I frowned, but the pleading look in Elaine's eyes told me to do what she requested. So I adjusted Destiny on my hip and did a slow spin as she studied me.

"Well, you obviously didn't grow up too poor," she said. "Because it looks like you've eaten well."

I turned back around to see if the comment made anyone else uncomfortable but if it did, no one seemed to react.

"I am Madeline Wingate," she said, extending her hand. "The matriarch of this family. And your," she paused as if her next words pained her, "your great-grandmother."

"It's nice to meet you," I said. I don't know why I felt reduced to a little girl standing before this woman. It was at that moment that I noticed the entire room had grown silent since she entered. Almost as if they were waiting on her to give her approval of my very existence.

She leaned in and looked at my daughter.

"This is Destiny, my baby," I said with a smile. With my daughter's rosy, plump cheeks, I wondered if Madeline would kiss them or stroke them, as that was usually what people instantly went toward. But instead, she stood back erect. "Destiny. What kind of name is that? It sounds worldly."

"Excuse me?" I said, again noticing how no one flinched.

"Grandmother, you know these kids today," Elaine interjected, releasing a fake chuckle. "They like to use fancy names."

"There is nothing fancy about that name," Mother Madeline said. "It's just ridiculous." She cocked her head and studied my daughter some more. "And do something with that child's hair," she ordered.

I ran my fingers through Destiny's wild 'fro and said, "What's wrong with my baby's hair?"

Mother Madeline shook her head, her nose turned up. "That nappiness is unacceptable. Put a . . . what is it that you all do?" She looked up like she was searching for the right term. "Put a perm in to straighten her hair. Do something," she said with disgust, "because that child's hair is a mess."

I was dumbfounded. "She's only eight months old. I'm not putting a relaxer on her head," I said.

"Hmph," she replied. "You need to do something, because no Wingate child needs to be walking around looking like that."

"Well, she can't walk, so there's that," I said, getting pissed. Not just at her comments, but at the silence in the room. "And she's not a Wingate. She's a Reed."

It was obvious no one ever dared challenge Mother Madeline. Even she looked stunned for a moment before saying, "Well, if you are who you say you are, Wingate blood runs through her veins."

My mouth fell open. "Wow. If I am who I say I am? The DNA test says I am the child of Elaine and Major Logan."

"Hmph," was her only response to that. She stiffened and glared at me. "Elaine, you'd better educate your long-lost *child* on the respect that is given in the Wingate family because her tone with me is totally unacceptable."

I waited for Elaine to step up and say something, but she remained quiet.

"Respect must be given in order to be gotten," I said.

"And this is why I have always been against inbreeding," she said, glaring at Elaine. "Their classless genes always dominate."

I couldn't believe her words—or the continuing silence.

"Wow, so my great-grandmother is a bigot. Glad I'm learning about my heritage," I said.

Gasps resonated across the room. But I didn't care. These people could be okay with this old lady's bigotry, but no way was I about to subject me or my daughter to this.

"What did you just say?" she said.

"Everyone else may be okay with your antiquated, racist ways, but I'm not. I don't know you and at this rate, I don't care to know you," I told her.

Mother Madeline put her hand to her chest in shock. "Catherine," she said, motioning to a woman who had been identified earlier as an aunt, "Take me out to the veranda. Your useless niece needs to teach this girl some manners." She turned to Elaine. "It should come as no surprise, though, that you birthed such a disrespectful child. You don't demand respect, not from her," she said, spitting out the reference to me, "and not from your philandering husband. It's no wonder she's a disrespectful twit."

Major, who was also off in the corner, gritted his teeth but didn't say a word. In fact, none of the twenty or so people in the room said anything as Catherine scurried to lead Mother Madeline out.

My husband's entrance broke the silent tension that hung in the room. "Hey, why is everyone looking so solemn?" he asked as he walked in the family room.

My anger was on overdrive.

"What's going on? What did I miss?" he asked.

I held my daughter tight as I steadied my breathing. Phillip, who was standing off in the corner, simply smirked and said, "Just another day in the Logan family."

"Babe?" Malcolm said.

"Get me out of here," I said. My mother had been right—there were some things that money couldn't buy.

Chapter 36

I tapped on the door and waited until I heard Elaine call out, "It's open, come on in."

I'd left right after that fiasco with Mother Madeline. Malcolm had managed to calm me down, then I had feigned a headache. Well, I didn't really have to fake it because the whole experience had sent my head to pounding.

This morning, I'd wanted to talk to Elaine, not just about that bigot of a woman she called her grandmother, but the "philandering husband" comment, which had bothered me all night. Not as much as the derogatory comments toward my daughter, but they were still very much unsettling.

I eased the bedroom door open and walked in to find Elaine sitting in a chaise in the corner of her room. Her smile lit up when she saw me. "Hello. How are you this morning?"

"I'm okay," I said. "That was . . . something last night."

A sympathetic expression crossed her face.

"I am really sorry about that. Mother Madeline can be . . . a lot," she said.

My thoughts replayed my mother's words: *I don't want you raised in that environment.* Had my mother saved me from a lifetime of that treatment?

"Well, I apologize if it didn't go like you wanted. I know that dinner meant a lot to you," I said.

"It was fine. The family got a chance to meet you. That's all that matters." She slapped her palms on her thighs and a wide smile crossed her face. "So what brings you by so bright and early?"

"I actually wanted to talk to you about the party. A few things—one, your grandmother is ninety. While that doesn't excuse her bad behavior, she's from a different era. But I don't understand why you, or no one else, stood up for me," I said.

"Our family dynamics are complicated," she said. "I know that Mother Madeline can be a little bigoted."

"You are either a bigot or you are not. There is no such thing as a little bigoted," I replied.

Elaine shrugged. "She's old. We just overlook her."

"That's unacceptable," I replied. "I guess we need to stay away from one another, because I will call her out."

Just the thought seemed to mortify Elaine.

I continued, "I am very easygoing—until it comes to my daughter. I will allow her to see for herself exactly what your grandmother is and I will show her what it means to stand against vitriol—even in one's own family—so that she knows how to stand against it in the world at large."

My words must've gotten to her because Elaine got quiet, then she said, "I wish that I had your strength back when you were a baby. My grandmother used to say vile things, and I just pushed them aside, telling myself you were too young to understand anyway."

I wanted to ask her what her plan had been for when I was old enough to understand. But I already knew the answer to that—she didn't have a plan.

"But I understand," she said. "And again, I deeply apologize."

She reached out to hug me and it wasn't until she released me that I noticed the pink bedspread and the dainty décor throughout the room. It was shocking that a man would be staying in this room.

Elaine must've noticed my expression because her smile faded and she said, "Yes, I live alone in this room."

"Oh," was the only thing I could think of to say.

"Have a seat," Elaine said, motioning to the small sofa that sat across from her bed. "I guess now that we have dealt with my grandmother's racist comments, I should explain her comments regarding Major." She sat back down on her chaise. "He told me what happened with Stephanie."

My mouth fell open. "You . . . you know about Stephanie?" I asked.

She rolled her eyes and let out a pained laugh. "Stephanie has been a thorn in my side for years. For some reason, she believes Major will," she made air quotes, "come to his senses and leave me." She motioned around the room. "Leave our home and marry her."

I was speechless. I didn't know what to say. "So, you're okay with my father having an affair?"

"My grandfather was a philanderer. Mother Madeline looked the other way. My mother looked the other way. And now, I look the other way."

"But why?" I asked.

She shrugged. "Men will be men. Just keep living. Marriage isn't about monogamy."

That caused my right eyebrow to rise.

"Oh, it's great if you can get it," she added. "But marriage is a contract. A business deal. And your father and I make some wonderful deals."

"Marriage is about love." I said, not believing that I was having this conversation. Is that why my mother didn't feel like Elaine deserved my father?

Elaine shook her head like I had so much to learn. "Love is all roses and dandelions . . . until you are tested." Her expression turned solemn. "Your kidnapping tested us." She shrugged nonchalantly. "And I suppose we failed. I withdrew and became a shell of my former self. And by the time I came out of my fog, my husband was seeking comfort in the arms of another woman."

"Wow. Stephanie has been around that long?"

She laughed again. "Oh, it wasn't Stephanie, sweetheart. It was someone else, then someone else. There's *always* someone else." I could hear the pain in her voice.

"And you're okay with that?"

She stared blankly at me. "It doesn't matter if I'm okay. Major did not sign up for," she pointed to a glass sitting on a small table next to the chaise, "this . . . me like this."

I thought about how my mother longed for a relationship with my father. Would he have done the same things to her that he had done to Elaine? I remember her telling me once as a little girl what I wished for wasn't always what I needed. I couldn't help but feel that was definitely applying to me now.

Elaine must have been gauging the look on my face.

"Oh, don't begrudge your father." She smiled and I saw the love in her eyes. "Men have needs. I recognize that and I no longer had the desire to meet any of those needs. So, what's a man to do?"

I shook my head, refusing to accept that. How could she possibly be all right with her husband seeing other women? "You all didn't want to go to counseling? Or do something to fix your relationship?" I asked.

"I'm fine with our relationship just as long as he keeps it respectful, then we have no problems," she confessed.

"Wow," I said. I hoped that I never get to that point in my life. I paused before my next question came out. "So, do you think if I had never been taken, things would have been different between the two of you?"

She shrugged again. "I don't know. We'll never know now, will we? But I will tell you this, your abduction altered our lives. So, that's where my bitterness comes from. That's why I can't let it go. Would we have been a happy family? Who knows. Every family has its own dysfunction, but that choice was taken away from me. Yes, we've had Phillip all our lives but Phillip isn't my child. Hell, he can't even stand me and is simply waiting for me to die." She released a pained sigh.

I couldn't argue with that. In fact, nothing about Phillip said he was capable of loving anyone.

"But think about what you feel for Destiny," she continued as she headed over to the floor to ceiling window in her bedroom. "A mother's love. That's what I felt for you." She was quiet as she looked outside over their massive, manicured backyard. "That's what I *feel* for you. It breaks my heart every time you refer to that woman as your mother." When she turned back to me, there were tears in her eyes. "I'll never understand or accept that. You want me to be okay with the woman who stole you from me. I know the contract stipulation upset you, but she has to pay one way or the other."

I nodded only because I didn't know what else to say or do. Her pain was palpable.

"I saw the way you were looking when Phillip and I were arguing. Or when my family, God bless their hearts, was being their usual obnoxious selves. But our bloodline is our bloodline. That's one thing we cannot change," she continued.

I thought about my mother and how she would've never disrespected me like Elaine did Phillip, she would've never disrespected anyone like that. For once, I understood what she meant when she used to say nurture is more important that nature.

"Honestly, if I was in your shoes, and someone took Destiny, I would be upset as well. So I understand where your anger and frustration is coming from," I told her. "But my mother is my mother. I can't change the circumstances of how she became my mother."

Elaine's whole body tensed up, so I took a step toward her and put a hand on her arm.

"I would like to get to know you better," I said. "I'd like to develop a relationship with you, but it can't be at her expense." I took a deep breath. My visit with my mother let me know that I couldn't go that long without seeing her again. I needed to stop straddling the fence and let Elaine know my mother would not be wiped out of my life. "So, if you wish to proceed to press charges, then my mother and I will fight them. We will get the best legal help we can find. Even if we have to go public and get someone to do it pro bono. But I will not turn my back on her, not for any amount of money." I reached into my pocket, pulled out the check and handed it back to her.

She didn't move to take it, simply looked at me as tears streamed down her face.

"It's up to you," I continued, setting the check on her dresser when she wouldn't take it. "Here's your check. If you want to file charges, fine. It won't change the fact that my family includes Connie Harrison. Now, I'd like my family to include you, too. So you think about it and let me know what you want to do."

I turned and walked out of the door, proud that I had done what my mother had done so many times for me, I'd stood up for her.

Chapter 37

It had been a week since I had given Elaine the check back. She had yet to say anything to me, so I could only assume that meant that she was planning on moving forward with pressing charges. If that's what she wanted, that's what she would get.

Malcolm had taken the news of my decision surprisingly well. He said he was standing by me, whatever I decided to do.

"Good morning, baby."

The smile on my husband's face brought me out of my thoughts. I had come up to his office to pick up the paperwork for the new house we were renting. After I'd told him about my conversation, he'd moved fast, found us a place and if everything checked out, we could move next week.

I gave my husband a quick peck. "I'll go drop this off with the realtor now."

"Great. Sorry I'm running, have to get into a meeting."

I loved seeing him in his element. And I could tell he loved being in it. The development team were excited about his app and were already working on the improvements, which gave Malcolm time to begin working on the prototype for another program.

I started checking my social media account as I waited on the elevator door to open. When I heard the ding, I stepped on, my gaze still on my phone, when I bumped right into Phillip.

He scowled at me and just mumbled, "Watch where you're going."

"Hello, Phillip," I said, stepping back.

He grunted, waved me off, and walked around me.

Since I was probably exiled from the Logan family, I figured I might as well go out with a bang. I was fed up with Phillip Logan and about to tell him about himself.

"Can I talk to you?" I said, following him down the hallway into his office.

"I'm quite busy."

"It will only take a minute," I said, closing the door behind me.

He sighed, like my mere existence was irritating. "What do you need, Jillian?" he asked as he walked around behind his huge cherry wood desk. It was funny, almost every other executive at Logan Industries had contemporary and sleek furniture. Phillip, who had to be the youngest executive on staff, had this antique looking décor.

I stepped in front of his desk. "From the day I met you, you've acted like I have been a thorn in your side and I need to know what your problem is with me," I said.

He shrugged like he had no idea what I was talking about. "I don't have a problem," he said as he began shuffling papers.

"No, you really do." I sat down in a wingback chair that reminded me of the ones at the Logans' home. "And I'm not going anywhere until you tell me what that problem is. I want to know where the disdain for me is coming from."

A smirk crossed his face as he took a seat as well. "Of course, the spoiled little rich girl is demanding her way. Everyone caters to her, so I should too."

"Are you for real?" I balked. "You know better than anyone else that's not true. After all, I grew up poor and struggling. You were living my life, so I think that's a moniker that would go to you."

He folded his arms, pursed his lips and leaned forward in his leather chair. "Your life? You know, you're right about that. I didn't ask to become the replacement child." His voice was pierced with anger. "I didn't ask for both of my parents to die in a frigging car crash. But that's exactly what happened. And you know what? My aunt and uncle stepped in so I thought I was going to be okay. I was just happy to have a family." He inhaled, I guess trying to keep himself from getting worked up. "Only I never really did have a family. Oh, I tried, God knows I tried, but I didn't have one. I had an aunt who was a shell of a person because her precious baby girl was gone. She never had time for anything because she was in mourning for years. She never came to a single game, a play, nothing."

I started to soften because the pain of his childhood was evident all over his face.

He leaned forward again, his tone stern. "Can you imagine what it's like growing up living in the shadow of this girl you never knew?" he asked. "Can you imagine drawing a picture for someone, being so proud of that picture, but when you show it to them, it causes them to burst into tears because it's a reminder that their precious baby girl will never draw them pictures? There were baby photos of you all over the house. We didn't have a picture of me until my senior year, when I put it up myself." He released a pained chuckle. "Do you know I burned a few of your baby pictures when I was twelve? Because I was sick of hearing about this perfect child. And you would've thought that I was the one who kidnapped you because Elaine refused to speak to me for three months over the torched pictures. I was a child. A damn child simply seeking love."

I suddenly felt bad about charging him up. "Is that why your relationship with Elaine is so contentious?"

"Our relationship is contentious because she's a mean old bitch," he countered. "To me, anyway." He took a deep breath as he leaned back. "But hey, the good thing is I quickly came to learn my position and I've played it very well."

"And is that your problem with me, you think I'm trying to push you out of your position and take your fortune?" I asked matter-of-factly.

He laughed. "Do you think that's all I want?" he asked. "I know that's what Aunt Elaine thinks, that I just want their fortune. I wanted more than money. I wanted love."

"Do you still want that?"

He shrugged nonchalantly. "I'm good. I became a hard ass because that's how I survived living with my aunt and uncle. My uncle tried, he really did. But he was always too busy. And then he started staying away from home, and I can't say that I blamed him. When Elaine lost you, she had nothing left to give."

I immediately regretted barging into his office. "I'm sorry, Phillip. I had no idea things were like that for you."

His tone softened. "Was I happy about them going to find you? No. I couldn't believe it. Maybe I didn't want to believe it. But you haunted my childhood."

"We're not children anymore," I told him.

He nodded and simply said, "I had no desire to bring you into my adult life either."

I stood. "Look, I'm here now. I'm not going anywhere." Even if the Logans decided to press charges against my mother, Malcolm was working here, so we needed to learn how to get along. But I didn't feel the need to give Phillip all of those details. "It doesn't have to be a competition."

He nodded, though he didn't reply.

"My mother, I mean, my . . ." I paused. In that moment, I decided to stop "othering" the woman who raised me. "My *mother* used to say 'a rising tide lifts all boats.' There is room for all of us to succeed and do well."

It surprised me, but a small smile crossed his face.

"My mother used to say that as well. I was so young I didn't know what it meant."

"See, we have more in common than you thought," I said with a grin.

His rigid demeanor softened and I felt like we'd just had a major breakthrough.

Chapter 38

It felt strange sitting in this church, with its structured service and choir singing monotone hymns. It was a far cry from the Baptist church I'd grown up in. But Elaine had finally talked to me and said she respected my decision, and had no plans to bring charges against my mother. I knew that took a lot, and I was so thrilled that when she asked me and Malcolm to bring Destiny to church service with her today, I'd felt like I didn't have any other choice

But now, I felt extremely uncomfortable sitting there like I'd been on display, especially when the priest had asked everyone to acknowledge me and thank God for my safe return. I felt like I was under a microscope, but I'd taken Malcolm's hand as he held Destiny and went to the front of the church.

The priest began, "As many of you know, the Wingates are longtime members of our church." He paused and looked down with reverence at Mother Madeline, who sat in the front row. "In fact, as many of you know, we wouldn't have that new organ were it not for the Wingate generosity."

She smiled her approval.

"And many of you know of the tragedy Major and Elaine Logan suffered many years ago. The horrible kidnapping of their baby daughter." He paused for effect. "Well, we are happy to report that their baby girl is home!" He motioned in our direction.

I smiled, but couldn't help but notice how Mother Madeline was looking at me with a scowl on her face.

We finished the services and headed out into the vestibule, where Mother Madeline was waiting. Her eyes went to Destiny who I was carrying on my hip.

"I can't believe you brought that baby out looking like a pickaninny."

My mouth fell open in shock. I'd had enough. I stepped toward my great-grandmother. "Mother Madeline, I know we just met and I know everyone around here—"

"Jill, please," Elaine said, stepping toward me and whispering a cautionary warning.

I jerked away from her. "No. That's part of the problem. You all give her a pass to say whatever she wants. No matter how rude and disrespectful it is. That's not okay."

"Excuse me," Mother Madeline said.

"I didn't stutter. It's obvious you dislike me."

"My, aren't we pompous today?" She folded her arms and smiled.

"You dislike at least fifty percent of me—the brown half. The half that invaded your pristine fairy tale to knock up your granddaughter."

Mother Madeline gasped and I immediately wished I hadn't gone there, but she'd pissed me off.

"You are a bigot and it's not okay."

"How dare you? I know some black people."

I sighed and shook my head. "That statement in and of itself is problematic. And the fact that you don't see that is disheartening."

Elaine's sister stepped toward me. "Please. Do not do this here. People are watching and I'm sure you're not aware, but we let our grandmother be herself."

I shook my head at her. "And your silence makes you just as guilty as she is. Your silence speaks volumes."

I turned back toward my great-grandmother. "I don't mean to disrespect you, even though everything you say to me is disrespectful. But I will not subject my daughter to this."

"I am just trying to prepare her for the world. She needs to be acclimated."

"By whose standards?"

"Society will judge her." She pointed to Destiny's curly 'fro. "Especially if she's walking about with her hair like that."

"What is wrong with the hair God gave her?" I asked.

I saved you from them.

My mother's words rang in my head. What if I had grown up around these people? Would I have a complex? Would I have been subjected to ridicule because of my own curly 'fro?

In that moment I realized that I had been so focused on all the positive things I missed, but judging from the family dynamics, there would've been a lot of negatives that would've shaped who I was as well.

I glanced around at the people who were trying to act like they weren't looking at us and decided nothing I said would matter to Mother Madeline. I'd told her how I felt and that was really all I could do.

"Come on, Malcolm," I said to my husband, and we headed out of the lobby of the church.

Phillip was standing near the door where we were exiting.

"What?" I snapped at him since he was just staring at me.

A slow smile spread across his face. "I guess you told her. It's about time someone did." Then he winked at me and walked away.

Chapter 39

"So with the projected growth, we are on tap to meet all of our 2021 goals. I'm extremely excited about the work our team has done." Phillip closed his notebook and flipped off the PowerPoint presentation as everyone at the table gave him a round of applause.

"Good job," said Barry Harris, the Vice President of Operations. "Don't you think so, Major?" He tapped my father's arm. He'd been busy reading emails on his phone.

"Huh?" Malcolm said.

"Phillip's presentation. It was right on point. He far exceeded our quarterly goals."

"Oh, yes. Good job, Phillip. Good meeting everyone." Major stood.

Phillip's lips were tight as he glared at Major. "Wasn't sure if you were listening."

"Of course I was. I've learned the art of multitasking." He glanced over at me. "Good meeting, everyone."

"I think we should go celebrate," Barry said. "This has been six months of hard work that Phillip has done and I think this is going to lead to big things for our company."

"Yes! Take the team out, on me," Major declared.

"You're not going to come?" Phillip asked.

"Nope, I have a date with my daughter this afternoon," Major said with a smile in my direction. I'd called and asked him to free his afternoon for me. He'd asked me to sit in on Phillip's presentation, then we could head out after that.

All eyes turned to me and I felt extremely uncomfortable, especially with the way Phillip was glaring at me.

"Mr. Logan, you don't think—"

"Are you ready to go, Jill?" he said to me, standing and extending his hand.

I nodded but took his hand and followed him out. I felt Phillip's eyes pierce my back as Major took my arm, placed it through his, and led me out of the conference room.

Thirty minutes later we were sitting inside McCormick and Schmick's Steakhouse. Major had ordered for both of us.

"I can't believe this is our first real one-on-one time. I don't know if I told you, but we are so happy to have you home," he said.

"Tell me what it was like when I was growing up, looking for me. I can only imagine how I would be if Destiny was out somewhere I didn't know."

A forlorn expression crossed his face. "I wouldn't wish that on my worst enemy. It's different to lose a child and have a funeral and put them to rest. It's the not knowing . . . that's a whole different heartache."

We made more small talk and I discovered that my father was a very funny man. I could see why the women fell for him.

"So," he said, his tone taking a serious turn after he'd just cracked a joke. "I want to talk to you about Stephanie."

I stared at him.

"I know you must think I'm an awful man."

"I don't think anything."

"Well, I'm not. Am I an unfaithful man? I am. I don't want to be, and I wish to God your mother could give me the things I need and want. But she long ago lost that desire."

I couldn't believe he was sitting here blaming Elaine for his in-fidelity.

"I don't know if you'll ever understand. But it's like, say you wake up one day and Malcolm isn't there. He exists, but that's it. I went four years without sex."

That made me cringe. I wasn't interested in hearing that.

"I don't mean to make you uncomfortable. I'm just trying to paint a picture for you. Your mother just shut me out. She shut the world out."

I wanted to remind him that he'd cheated on my mother, so to me it was a pattern.

He must've been reading my mind because he said, "What I did in college was dumb and stupid but it wasn't a reflection of the man that I was. In fact, it taught me to be wary of playing with women's hearts. So what I tried to do was just make sure that I gave my wife everything that she needed. Unfortunately, after a while, I got tired of trying. I had my first affair on your tenth birthday. Ten years of living with a zombie was about all I could take. Doesn't make it right, but it is what it is."

"Why didn't you all go to counseling?"

"I pleaded with your mother to do counseling, but she didn't want to. So we just learned to exist. I love her. I really do. I just wish that I could have her back."

He reached across the table and patted my hand. "And maybe now that you're here, I can."

I truly enjoyed the rest of our lunch, mentally preparing myself for part two of my afternoon with my father.

———✦———

"So you're really not going to tell me where we are going?"

I kept my gaze on the road ahead as my father sat in the pas-senger seat next to me.

"Dad, just ride and see, please?"

It was kind of strange. It hadn't been hard to acknowledge him as my father. Maybe because I'd never had one of those. I didn't know when, if ever, I'd be able to fully acknowledge Elaine as my mother.

My father had been elated at the request to accompany me on a drive. I don't know if he thought because of his racist in-laws and our moving out that I would cut him off, too. But I'd assured him that wasn't the case.

When he'd first asked where we were going, I'd told him it was a surprise. I think he was just happy I wanted to spend time with him, so he let it drop. But I guess after thirty minutes in the car, he was ready to have some answers.

"This is crazy, Jill. I want to know where we're going and why you couldn't have Lance drive?" he said, referring to his driver.

I looked over and flashed a warm smile at him. "Because I wanted it to be just the two of us."

That seemed to settle him and he said, "Okay. But you could be driving me off a cliff or something."

"Trust me, I'm not. I'll tell you where we're going when we get there," I said.

I could tell he wasn't used to relinquishing control, but he leaned back and waited as I navigated along the freeway. We were in my Ford Festiva, but if it bothered him, he didn't let on.

I had debated this move for days, especially because I didn't know how he'd react. But then, I decided to just go for it. It was way past time.

After a few minutes of silence in the car, I said, "So, Dad, can I ask you a question?"

"Yes, you can ask me anything."

"What's the deal with Phillip?"

"What do you mean?"

"I think I've reached an understanding with him, but I'm wondering if he's worried I'll take all your money and there will be nothing left for him?" I looked over at him. "I want you to know that I don't want your money."

My father chuckled. "Everybody wants money. But I know that's not what you're after. And deep down, Phillip knows it too." He patted my hand. "Don't worry about Phillip. I promised my sister that he would be well taken care of and he is." My father leaned back in his seat. "Phillip is very high strung. Instead of letting things flow naturally, he tries to force it. And he severely lacks social skills. But I do imagine we are to blame for that. When my sister passed, he came to us and neither your mother nor I was really in a position to be a nurturer. So Phillip kind of found his own way."

I nodded my understanding. His words matched what Phillip said about his childhood. "Well, you might want to let him know you won't leave him broke. That might make everything smoother between all of us."

Once I reached my exit, I made a quick right turn and headed in the direction of the home.

My father leaned in, studied the name on the sign out front. "Um, why are we here?" he said, looking from the sign to the building that I had just parked in front of.

I turned the car off, then shifted my body so that I was facing him. My tone was serious because I wanted him to understand how serious this was. "You acknowledge that you had a relationship with my mother."

"Yes, but . . ."

"But in the end, the reality is that you left her," I said.

Regret filled my father's face. "I was young and dumb, Jill," he said. Then he looked around. "What is this place?"

"It is the facility where my mother now lives."

He was silent. "They told me it was nice." He leaned in and peered out the window. "I'm glad." But then he turned back to face me. "Why are we here?" he asked.

"Because you need to face her," I replied. "Because I can't be whole until the halves of me that are broken are fixed. You both have anger and bitterness that will never go away until you face one another."

"I don't know about this, Jill," he said. "I haven't seen your mother in almost thirty years. I just don't think this is a good idea."

"Well, I do," I said, turning the car off then stepping out the driver's side door. For a minute I didn't think he was going to get out. But after a brief hesitation, he opened the door and followed me inside. I said hello to the receptionist. And she waved back.

"You're here for Ms. Connie, right?" she said.

"Yes," I replied, surprised that she remembered since I'd only been here twice—the day I dropped her off and the day I came to visit.

"Your mom is in a mood today," she said, her eyes suddenly lighting up when she saw my father. "Hello," she said.

My father was nervous and not receptive to her flirtatious greeting. "Hi," he said before turning to me. "Maybe you should go on and do this yourself."

"We're here now. Come on." I took his hand and led him down the hallway toward her room. Once again, the door was cracked, so I tapped then walked in.

"Mama?" I said.

She was in the rocking chair and once again kept her back to me. "I would think that someone was in my room talking to me. But, I'm no one's mother," she said, as she rocked back and forth.

"Mama, I brought someone with me," I said.

She turned around and I could tell by the look on her face that today was a clear-mind day. Oh, the anger was evident, but at the sight of my father standing next to me, all traces of anger disappeared.

"Major?" she whispered in shock.

He shifted uncomfortably. And then said, "Virginia."

"Oh my God, Major. What are you doing here?" My mother's eyes darted to me and I saw a wave of fear rush over her face. "Did you come to take me to jail?" She gripped the handles of her rocking chair like she was preparing to make a run for it. Where, I had no idea.

"I'd like to know what I'm doing here myself," he said, looking at me.

"I need you two to see each other. Mama," I said, turning to her, "I need you to see what you did to him. And," I paused, "Dad, I need you to see what your abandonment and betrayal did to her."

An awkward silence hung in the air. But at least my mother stopped rocking. Finally, she said, "You're a liar and a cheat."

"And you're a kidnapper," he retorted without hesitation.

It was as if I was no longer in the room as their venomous glares pierced each other.

"My child was stolen. Taken from me," my mother said. "Probably because you prayed and prayed for that to happen."

"Don't be ridiculous," he said. "I didn't want children, but I didn't pray for our child to die."

"You wanted me to get an abortion," she replied. "That was the first thing that came to your mind. You never even thought about raising our child."

"And as I told Jillian, I have regretted that ever since," my father said. "I carried that guilt deep down inside since. I didn't want the child, God took him from me."

She stared at him as her eyes pooled. "It was a her."

My father looked pained that he didn't know that.

"I buried her alone. While you danced over her death, I buried her alone. The only child I would ever conceive," my mother said.

"Why in the world would you say I danced over her death?" he replied. "I had mixed emotions. My child had died and I felt guilt that I'd never even felt it, felt *her*, kick."

"You grieved for our child?" my mother asked in surprise.

"Of course. I know you want to believe I was some type of monster, but I wasn't. I was a kid who made a mistake. I liked you a whole lot, but I was in love with Elaine."

That looked like it hurt her as much as it did almost thirty years ago.

"I'm so sorry," my father said. "I never meant to cause you that type of pain."

I thought his apology would send my mother into tears, but instead, she simply nodded and swallowed back the tears that were threatening to escape.

"I'm sorry I took her," my mother finally said. She resumed rocking. "And if you and your wife want me to pay by having me live what little life I have left behind bars, then so be it. My daughter has turned her back on me, so I don't have a life worth living anymore anyway."

Those words pained me, but I couldn't allow my mother's guilt to suck me into submission.

"I wanted you here," I told my father, "so that both of you could make peace. This woman here," I touched my mother's shoulder, "is my mother. It doesn't matter how she got the title, it's the title she bears." I lifted my mother's chin. "Yes, I put you in this facility, but I'm not going anywhere." I hugged her and felt her relief. I then stood up and faced Major. "Now, I understand the conditions of the agreements and I want you to understand, I do not want to do this. But I've thought long and hard about this. Logan Industries can't use any negative publicity. If you demand that I cut myself off from my mother, I may have to give Oprah our story."

"What? You know Oprah?" my mom asked.

"You would publicly embarrass us like that?" my father asked, horrified at my declaration.

"I would do whatever it takes to keep my relationship with my mother intact," I replied.

"But—"

"No, I need you to understand that," I said, cutting him off. "I will respect your wife, my biological mother, but I can't cut out the mother who raised me. So we're all going to have to find a way to get along."

I glanced at both of my parents and was glad to see them nodding their heads in agreement.

Chapter 40

I was living a double life. I guess that was poetic because that's what my whole life had been. The life I lived and the life I should have lived.

It had been a month since I took my father to see my mother and I'd spent that time trying to come to terms with the lie that had been my life. I'd forgiven Elaine for not watching me, and my mother for taking me. I knew that there was no way I could focus on my future if I was still caught up in the past.

I no longer found myself wondering what if I had grown up as a Logan. The fact was, I had grown up a Harrison. It might've been a commandeered name, but it was my name. It was who I was.

I recognize that my mother needed to pay for her crime. But when I said that she has, I meant it. She sacrificed her life—never getting married, feeling like since she'd taken me, her life should be spent dedicated to mine. And the dementia, which over the last two weeks had returned with hurricane strength, had destroyed her future, so I needed to treasure the time that I had with her. I also recognized that from that one wrongdoing, I was given the best life. I might not have had everything I ever wanted, but I never went without the things that I needed. For that, I would forever be grateful.

"It looks really good in here."

I turned toward the sound of Elaine's voice. She'd come over to the new house to watch Destiny as I unpacked. Of course, she'd been heartbroken when we moved into our own place, but I needed my own. And with the acquisition payment my husband had received for his app, we were able to get it. I didn't want to wait on a home to be built, so we'd found this amazing four-thousand-square-foot home that I hoped to one day fill with children.

"Thanks," I said. "You were right. It was fun shopping for new furniture."

"Ahh, you have some Wingate traits after all." Elaine winked. Then her gaze drifted toward the picture on the mantel, of both my mothers.

I didn't expect Elaine to ever forgive my mother, but her lifetime of anger had already cost her so much. My hope was that she could release it and I wanted her to no longer dwell on the past but work toward the future.

I braced myself for her to comment. But she simply pursed her lips and didn't say a word. That, in and of itself, was progress.

She looked away from the picture.

"I'm going to take Destiny to the park." She caught herself. "*May* I take Destiny to the park?" she corrected.

"I think she would love that," I said with a smile.

Her expression turned serious as she said, "I promise to pay attention so that nothing happens to her."

"I know you will." If I didn't know anything else, I knew that she wouldn't let Destiny out of her sight.

Elaine tucked my daughter in the stroller, then leaned in and kissed her plump cheeks. She stood and looked at me. "Thank you. For not shutting me out. I should've never made the demand that you cut off . . . that you have nothing to do . . . with her."

I smiled as I wondered if Elaine would ever be able to say my mother's name.

"It's okay. I understand why you did it. I really do. I don't know how I would react if someone did the same thing to Destiny, so I get it. But what I want you to do is forgive her—and yourself."

She took a deep breath. "I lost so much because I couldn't let the anger go."

"I know." I hesitated, trying to decide if I was going to address her issues with my father. He needed her to want to be his wife—something she had long ago stopped doing.

"You do know that you deserve happiness, right?"

She sighed. "I know Major wants to give it to me. I just have shut him out for so long, I don't know any other way."

"I once saw a motivational speaker at one of our Starbucks trainings. She said that when it comes to making decisions in our lives, we should look at it as a fork in the road. I know this sounds cheesy, but look as life as a journey. On this journey, there are many possible paths to take and many forks in the road. You're standing at one of those forks right now. Either do what you've always been doing and keep getting what you've always been getting, or do something different and get different results. You cannot continue to beat yourself up for what happened. Release it," I said.

She hugged me tightly. "I'm going to try. I'm so grateful God brought you back to me." She stepped back and walked back over to Destiny. "So, how long will you be gone?"

"Just a few hours," I replied. I didn't go into details, but Elaine knew that my Saturday mornings were spent with my other mother. I had to let my own guilt about having her in that facility go. My mother was in a place that was giving her care that I could not. I had come to terms with that.

We could afford to get her a live-in caregiver, but right now, this was what was best for her. The six-figure check was in the bank, cashed with no stipulations, earning interest and waiting on us to put it to good use. For now, I was content. I didn't need riches. My mother—Connie, had shown me that.

I had learned to be appreciative of the little things, like the fact that I now knew where I got my physical appearance from. It's good to know, or at least see, the physical reflection of your genetics in another person. It is something that I grew up never having, but now that I have experienced it, I would never trade it for the world.

I kissed my daughter goodbye, then leaned in, and did something I had never done before. I kissed my mother on the cheek. Her tears were immediate.

"Thank you," she said.

I smiled, waved goodbye, then gathered my things to go spend time with my other mother.

A Note from the Author

Well, I've done it again. Completed yet another book—my fifty-first. When I started this one, I told myself, 'Girl, you've written fifty-one books. Who else could you possibly acknowledge?' But here's the thing, each book is crafted from a different journey. And different people who help make it possible. (Of course, my core group has been there since Day One.) So I guess you guys will just have to bear with me as I continue to pay homage to the folks who help me do what I do.

The acknowledgments, or Note from the Author, as I like to call it, well that one isn't so easy. Particularly because I wouldn't be where I am today if it weren't for some really fantastic people. And since I'm not trying to create Encyclopedia Billingsley, I simply can't name them all. But bear with me as I try to recognize JUST A FEW of the people who make what I do possible.

I've been blessed to have a long and somewhat successful career doing what I love. I wouldn't be able to do what I love were it not for all the people who are always in my corner.

Major love to my amazing and patient family. Though you long ago stopped being impressed with my new books, your support has never wavered. My children—the lights of my—Mya, Morgan, and Myles—I love you to the moon and beyond. Special shout-out to Tanisha Tate, my sister, my soror, my friend. I am so blessed to have you in my life.

My business partner, writing partner, therapist, voice of reason, and friend-till-the-end, Victoria Christopher Murray.

My core . . . my forever ride-or-die friends who stopped reading at book number two, but never stopped supporting: Jaimi Canady, Raquelle Lewis, Kim Wright, and Clemelia Humphrey Richardson . . . thirty-plus years and we're still going strong.

To my muse, who makes me smile . . . who makes me pause . . . and just enjoy life . . . my #1 draft pick . . . Jeffrey Caradine, I'm so grateful that God brought you into my life.

To my BGB admin family: Jason, Kimyatta . . . thank you so much for all that you do. To our amazing partners . . . I'm thrilled you're still going strong with us. And of course I have to shout out Pat Tucker for simply being a friend.

As usual, thanks to my agent since day one, Sara Camilli; my editors Selena James, Rebecca, and Esi, and the entire team at Kensington Books.

Major love to all the amazing book clubs that have supported me since my first book and the onces who have discovered me along the way.

Thank you to all the wonderful libraries that have also supported my books, introduced me to readers, and fought to get my books on the shelves.

Thank you to my friends and family on social media. Yes, for many of us, we've never met, but I'm eternally grateful for all of your support and encouragement.

Lots of love and gratitude to my sorors of Alpha Kappa Alpha Sorority Inc. (including my own chapter, Mu Kappa Omega), my sisters in Greekdom, Delta Sigma Theta Sorority Inc., who *constantly* show me love . . . and my fellow mothers in Jack and Jill of America, especially the Missouri City/Sugar Land chapter.

And finally thanks to YOU . . . my beloved reader. If it's your first time picking up one of my books, I truly hope you enjoy. If you're coming back, words cannot even begin to express how eternally grateful I am for your support. From the bottom of my heart, thank you!

Much Love,
ReShonda

DON'T MISS

In this stunning sequel to her acclaimed debut *My Brother's Keeper*, #1 national bestselling author ReShonda Tate Billingsley brings her real-deal insight to a heartfelt new novel about a wife and mother on a daring rescue mission—to save herself.

More to Life

Enjoy the following excerpt from *More to Life* . . .

Chapter 1

Living my best life!

That thought made me wiggle, shimmy, and shake. That was what I was about to finally do. No more back burner livin' for me. After years of putting my dreams on hold, I was about to step out.

"And I'm gonna do more than just step out," I said to my reflection as I spread the Fenty gloss over my lips, then smacked them together. I stepped back, gave a girlfriend snap, and added, "I'm about to do me."

And it was going to begin with Oprah. While I'd made sure my family had a Christmas to remember, I had given myself the best gift ever—tickets to the exclusive "Living Your Best Life" one-day conference with Oprah as the opening speaker. The conference promised to help you "reconnect with your passion so you could walk in your purpose." This was going to be life-changing for me.

I hooked my earrings in place, fluffed out my natural curls, propped up my girls, then admired how the magenta Diane Von Furstenberg wrap dress brought out my golden overtone and gave me a glow.

I glanced at my watch: 7:57. I was making good time. "Today is going to be a good day," I sang as I grabbed my purse and headed out of the room.

I started humming as I headed down the stairs. "I'm doing me!" I said as I hit the bottom step, almost colliding with my son as he came around the corner.

"Really, Ma?" Eric moved his bowl of cereal to keep it from spilling.

I squeezed his chin. "Good morning, my handsome son." Eric was in his junior year at college and over the past year had become the spitting image of his father.

He pulled away and cocked his head. "Um, what's wrong with you?"

"I'm in a spectacular mood, that's all." I did another shimmy.

"Can you not?" He laughed as he headed into the kitchen.

I was about to ask him why he was walking around the house with a giant bowl of cereal, but before I could say anything, the front door opened and my daughter, Anika, came bouncing in. As the baby of the family, she commanded attention whenever she walked in the room, so trying to hold a conversation with Eric would've been moot anyway.

"Hey, Mom," she said.

"Hello, sweetheart," I replied. "You're out early."

"I had to go pick up Kelli from the airport, remember?" she said, motioning to one of her Spelman classmates who was walking in behind her. "I took your car because Dad said my car won't be out of the shop until tomorrow." She handed me my keys.

I extended my hand to the young Kerry Washington-look-alike who resembled my daughter so much it was eerie.

"Hello, Kelli," I said. "Anika has been so excited about your visit."

They giggled and hugged each other. "I'm excited, too," Kelli said. "My dad remarried and moved here and I did not want to spend the holidays with my stepmom. She's like only five years older than me. So thank you so much for letting me stay here a couple of days. I wish I could stay the whole break, but I have to go take part in the family drama." She released a disgusted chuckle.

Family drama. I knew all about that. Well, I used to when I was growing up. *No.* I shook off those thoughts. Memories were not about to mess up my day.

"Well, any friend of my daughter is a friend of mine," I said.

Kelli set her bag down and walked into our spacious entryway. Her mouth dropped open at the double winding staircase and large crystal chandelier that hung in the center. "Your home is beautiful," she said, taking in the surroundings. "And your Christmas tree. How tall is it?"

"Nine feet," I said. "And thank you so much for the compliment." I cut my eyes at Anika. "Maybe you can help my daughter take the tree and other Christmas decorations down this weekend."

"You know you like the stuff stored a certain way, so I wouldn't want to mess that up." She batted her eyes like she was doing me a favor.

Kelli continued surveying the house. I understood her awe, though. I'd worked hard to make our six-thousand-square-foot home a showcase. I'd imported tile from Tijuana, flown in drapes from Dubai, and bought furnishings from Finland. Our home had even been featured in a *Texas Monthly* "Best Homes" feature story.

"This place looks like it could be an art gallery," Kelli said.

That made my smile widen. My work . . . in an art gallery? That would be a dream come true. I wanted someone to be moved by my creations, to appreciate how I pour my soul onto the canvas. Shoot, at this point, I just wanted to create, do something that brought me personal joy. That's what I wanted to walk away from Oprah's conference with today—the inspiration to live my best life because I wasn't doing it right now.

Oh, I loved my family, but I wanted a life where my passion to paint could coexist. I hadn't found that yet. But now that both kids were in college, I definitely felt like it was my time.

"Oh my goodness. Is this a Jean-Michel Basquiat?" Kelli asked.

Anika burst out laughing. "That is hilarious. No, that's an Aja Clayton, my mom. It's her little hobby."

I grimaced at the dismissive way my daughter spoke of the thing that gave me my greatest joy outside of my family. But she'd come by it honestly. Her brother did it, her father did it. And when her grandmother, Judy—Charles's mother—had moved in several months ago, she'd fallen in line and started doing it, too. I guess the fact that I just did painting on the side made them see it as nothing more than a hobby. But it was my passion, even if it was buried underneath the weight of my world.

"I'm impressed that you know Basquiat," I said, deciding to do what I always did and ignore the condescending remark.

"Yes, he and LaTerus, the Modern Renaissance painter from Harlem, are my favorites. I'm an art history major," Kelli said.

That warmed my heart to see someone share my passion. I'd been painting since I was a little girl. It was my escape from the dysfunction that was my life. I'd wanted to major in art but my guidance counselor, who was helping me fill out my college paperwork, had come right out and said, "Be realistic, Aja. Major in something real."

I'd cried myself to sleep that night, then selected social work as my major.

Now watching Kelli take in my work confirmed that had been the worst choice I'd ever made.

"Wow, you could make a living off this," Kelli said, looking at another painting that hung over the entryway table.

"Yeah, right," Eric said, emerging from the dining room. "They're called starving artists for a reason, and all this," he said, pointing to his athletic body, "and starving doesn't go together." He laughed.

"Kelli, that's my bigheaded brother, Eric," Anika said.

Eric walked over, took Kelli's hand, and lifted it to his lips.

"Hello, beautiful," he said with the same charisma that made me fall for his father.

"Don't even think about it," Anika said, pulling her friend's arm and pushing her brother away.

"What? I'm just trying to be hospitable to your guest." Eric chuckled.

"Can you two save this fight for another time?" I said. "Kelli, make yourself at home. I have to get out of here for my conference."

"Where are you going?" Anika and Eric asked simultaneously.

I inhaled. Exhaled. Reminded myself this was going to be a good day.

"So I guess neither of you noticed that I'm dressed up." I pointed to my outfit.

They both looked me up and down. "Oh," they said in unison.

"My conference is today," I said. "The one I've been talking about for the past two weeks."

"Oh, that's right. You have that entrepreneur thingy. I forgot about that," Anika said. "Good thing we didn't stop on the way back." She turned to Kelli. "Talk about a scam. My mom is going to this conference where they get people to shell out $1,500 for a ticket so they can tell you stuff you already know."

I wasn't about to get into a debate with my children. Another glance at my watch. 8:08. I wanted to be in place by 9:30 since the conference started at ten. "Whatever. I'm heading out because I can't be late. There's no late entry."

Eric shrugged his indifference as he continued into the kitchen. I followed so I could grab a quick cup of coffee and some fruit.

"Okay, Mom," Anika said, following behind me. "But can you make us some of your homemade pancakes before you go?"

Any other time, I would've jumped at the chance to cook for my daughter and her guest. But not today.

"What part of I have to go do you not get?" I asked.

"Mom . . ."

I ignored her as I opened the cabinet and pulled out my coffee pod, then dropped it in the machine.

Eric set his bowl in the sink, with the dishes from last night that Anika hadn't bothered to wash. "Mom, did you fill out my immunization papers? They're due at noon," he said.

"So we're really not getting pancakes?" Anika asked.

I cut my eyes at her and she huffed.

"Can you get us an Uber to go to IHOP, then?" she asked. "My Uber app isn't working." She looked at her brother. "Or Eric can take us."

"I'm going back to bed. Besides, I don't have any gas."

Anika's eyes widened. "Ooh, speaking of gas. You're probably going to need some," she told me. "The light is on in your car."

"You brought my car back on empty?" I said, exasperation creeping in.

Anika just gave me a blank look and a "Sorry." She paused. "So no Uber either, huh?"

I took a deep breath. Now I was going to have to stop for gas. Thankfully, the convention center was only thirty minutes away, so I was still good. "Anika, you are more than capable of making you guys some breakfast."

"Fine. Come on, Kelli. I guess we'll just have to starve." She took her friend's hand and led her out of the kitchen.

"Mom," Eric said, "my paperwork?"

I sighed. I had meant to print that yesterday, but I'd had to go to Office Depot and get a new cartridge, and when I'd come home, the dog had chewed up one of my favorite shoes so I'd gotten distracted.

"No, I didn't get a chance to do it," I said. "Can't you do it?"

"Mom . . ."

I pressed the Start button on the Keurig. "Get your dad to do it. It's his insurance information. I really need to go."

"You know Dad doesn't know how to do that," Eric replied.

"Your dad doesn't know how to do what?"

I managed a smile when the love of my life walked in and planted a kiss on my cheek. Even in his running gear and his face covered with a layer of sweat, he looked like he needed to be modeling Under Armour gear in a magazine.

"How was your run?" I asked.

"Good. And Dad doesn't know what?" he repeated.

"Eric needs his immunization paperwork filled out," I said.

"Coach said if I don't have it in today by noon, I won't be able to play in the first game when we get back to school."

"Oh," Charles said. "That's a mom problem." He laughed like he'd really said something funny. "Babe, have you seen my driver? I have to be at the golf club in thirty minutes. I'm playing with the new Texans owner, and since I'm trying to snag that exclusive interview, I can't be late."

It was now 8:20. I wanted to tell him I couldn't be late either. But I just said, "Did you put it back in your bag after your game last week?"

"I could've sworn I did. But it's not there. Can you help me find it?" His voice was suddenly filled with frustration like he'd expected to walk right in here and I was going to tell him exactly where the driver was.

I shook my head. "I can't. I have to get to my event. The Oprah workshop."

"Oh. Is that today?"

I bit my bottom lip as I felt my enthusiasm waning. While what everyone else did was important to me, nothing I did seemed important to my family.

"I really need to get dressed," Charles said. "Can you help me look?"

"No," I repeated, keeping my voice even. "I have to get going. The event starts in an hour and a half and I want to be there early."

He eased up behind me, wrapped his arm around my waist, and kissed me on my neck. "Please?"

"Can you guys get a room," Eric groaned. "Mom, can you at least hook up the printer and print out the paperwork since you're making me figure this out on my own? I have to get it in by noon and you won't be back by then."

"You're a college student. You should know technology." I gently kissed my husband on the lips as I pushed him away. His kiss normally had a way of relaxing me, but today it wasn't working.

"No, I go to the computer lab and the printers are already hooked up," Eric said. "I don't even know where the cartridges are."

"Fine," I said. "I'll at least get the paperwork printed, but you're going to have to fill it out."

I ignored his groans as I headed to the office. "Just relax," I mumbled to myself. "You're good on time."

I grabbed the Office Depot bag, pulled the cartridge out, opened it, and replaced the old one. I released silent curses as I waited for my email to pop open so that I could print the immunization paperwork Eric's coach had sent.

"Finally," I mumbled as the PDF opened and I pressed Print. I had just reached to remove the paperwork when I noticed Charles's silver golf club in the corner of the office.

I sighed as I called out for my husband. "Charles! I found your driver."

I heard footsteps as he came racing down the hall. "Where was it?"

"For some reason you dropped it off in here." I pointed to the corner.

He snapped his finger. "Oh, yeah. I stepped in here for a call the last time I came from golfing." Charles leaned in and kissed me. "I knew you'd find it."

"Did you even look?" My voice had way more irritation than normal.

"Why are you snapping?"

I took a deep breath. "I'm sorry. It's just that this conference is very important to me and I feel like no one cares."

"Okay, you're being a little dramatic," he said with a smile. "We all care. I'm so glad you're leaving for your vacation in two days. You seem like you really need it. And I'm making sure you have the best birthday girl's trip ever, so don't get stressed."

"Okay, you're right." I released a slow breath.

"Come here, let me massage you." Charles pulled the rolling chair toward him.

A moan escaped me as Charles began kneading my shoulders. "Charles, I don't have time. And I thought you had to go, too."

"Oh, his assistant texted me. He pushed back our start time thirty minutes." He glanced at his watch. "But it is five till nine, so let me get out of here."

Five till nine? I wanted to scream. How had the time gotten away?

"Dangit," I muttered, swiveling around in the chair to pull the paperwork off the printer.

"Well, have fun at your event, babe." Charles leaned in to kiss me again. But he bumped my cup of coffee before making contact, and hot coffee spilled all over my dress and the paperwork I'd just printed.

"Are you freakin' kidding me?" I screamed as I jumped up.

Charles grabbed a Kleenex and immediately began rubbing.

"Stop! You're making it worse," I said. Charles backed away at my outburst. "It's fine. I'm fine. Just let me reprint this paperwork and go find something else to wear."

Charles eased out of the room and I prayed that I could get the papers printed, change my clothes, and get downtown in the next hour.

———◆———

It was 9:45 and my heart was pounding.

My dream was fifteen minutes away from being deferred. Again.

"Come on, come on, come on!" I screamed at the car in front of me. I pounded the steering wheel as I screamed at the little old lady who couldn't decide if she was going to go left or right.

I'd stopped for gas—rushing so I'd only put $5 in, which hadn't even turned my warning light off. But I just needed enough gas to get downtown.

If I miss this conference because of my family . . .

I pushed down the lump in my throat and the mist trying to cover my eyes as I glanced down at the GPS. I knew the way to the convention center but had turned on the GPS just to track my time. It had my arrival as 10:19, and I was praying that I'd be able to shave off some time.

My prayers hadn't been answered.

"Move!" I screamed at another car that had cut me off and slowed my speed race by twenty miles an hour.

"Breathe, Aja. Breathe," I mumbled. I'd been talking to myself the whole ride, trying my best to keep my nerves in check. "I know they stressed no late entries, but they'll have a grace period."

They have to have a grace period.

The GPS had been right on target because it was 10:19 when I pulled into the parking garage of the convention center. My hands were shaking in nervous anticipation. I drove around the second floor, and all the parking spots were taken, so I drove up to the third floor. After circling around and watching the clock on my dashboard turn to 10:26, I pulled into a handicapped space.

"Screw it," I said, deciding I'd just have to pay the ticket if I got one.

I parked and prayed for a miracle as I darted through the garage, across the skywalk, and into the auditorium.

The check-in desk was empty and my heart dropped.

"Excuse me," I said to a woman I saw standing at a table near the second entry. "I'm here for the 'Living Your Best Life' event. I'm registered." I fumbled for my phone to pull up my ticket.

The woman looked at her phone like she wanted to remind me of the time. I wanted to scream that I knew what time it was. "I am so sorry," she said. "There's no late entry. They've already started filming."

My chest began heaving. "Is . . . is there any way they can let me in?"

She flashed a sympathetic look. "I am so sorry," the woman repeated. "We even gave a fifteen-minute grace period. But that's why we have you submit the waiver, so we can make sure you are clear on the policy."

I wanted to explain to her my hectic morning, ask her if she was a mother and wife and understood how families could suck the breath out of you. Maybe if she could relate . . .

"I can submit a request to see if they'll give you a partial refund." She had the nerve to smile.

"I don't want a refund." My voice cracked. "I just want to go in."

The woman patted my hand. "I'm sorry. There's nothing I can do."

I nodded, unable to form a "Thank you anyway" as I scurried to the ladies' room. I dipped in a stall as my chest heaved. I'd never had a panic attack, but I imagined this was what one felt like.

Every time I tried to do something for me, something happened. Every time I took two steps forward, life pushed me three steps back. All my life, I'd given everything I had to my family. All I wanted was this . . . this day.

I'd obviously wanted too much.

I buried my face in my hands and sobbed.

Printed in the United States
by Baker & Taylor Publisher Services